# Icelandic MAGIC

"In many ways *Icelandic Magic* is as awe-inspiring and mysterious as the Icelandic landscape itself. Full of fascinating accounts of Iceland's magical history and grimoires, this book offers pragmatic instructions to resurrect this magic and tap into its power, yet there is a creative aspect that will inherently force the practitioner to union with their own inner sage. Flowers guides us safely through the ancient secrets of Icelandic magic into our own 'circuit boards of consciousness,' which we learn may be rewired through systematically formed staves aligned with our will."

SERA TIMMS, MUSICIAN, VISUAL ARTIST, PRIESTESS, AND LEAD VOCALIST OF BLACK MARE

"*Icelandic Magic* is a modern classic of Northern sorcery. Stephen Flowers's galdor-stave system exposes the frosty roots of sigil-working, revealing a magic available to anyone possessing pen, paper, and a hunger for transformation."

CLINT MARSH, AUTHOR OF *THE MENTALIST'S HANDBOOK*

"Stephen Flowers offers readers a comprehensive and erudite guide to the runes, staves, and other elements of Icelandic magic. This book opens the secret lore of Icelandic magicians for today's readers."

DAN HARMS, LIBRARIAN AT SUNY CORTLAND MEMORIAL LIBRARY, EDITOR OF *THE LONG-LOST FRIEND: A 19TH CENTURY AMERICAN GRIMOIRE,* AND AUTHOR OF *THE CTHULHU MYTHOS ENCYCLOPEDIA: A GUIDE TO H. P. LOVECRAFT'S UNIVERSE*

"In his latest work, Stephen E. Flowers pours forth his inspiration again. On the basis of sound, academic research, he provides a good basis for the praxis of Icelandic magic. The most important aspect of his teaching is that he defines the attitude and preparation necessary to become a sorcerer in the old tradition. A book by a magician, for magicians."

Christopher Alan Smith,
author of *Icelandic Magic: Aims, Tools and Techniques of the Icelandic Sorcerers*

"*Icelandic Magic* is an exciting new expansion that goes far beyond Flowers's previous Galdrabók. Much more than a presentation of historical grimoire material, Flowers goes on to identify the key components of the techniques and show readers how to construct their own workings in a traditional manner. *Icelandic Magic* explores both the inner and outer nature of galdor, and of magic in general, to give the reader the tools for gaining knowledge, wisdom, and self-transformation."

Alice Karlsdóttir, author of *Norse Goddess Magic*

# Icelandic MAGIC

## *Practical Secrets of the Northern Grimoires*

STEPHEN E. FLOWERS, Ph.D.

Inner Traditions
Rochester, Vermont • Toronto, Canada

Inner Traditions
One Park Street
Rochester, Vermont 05767
www.InnerTraditions.com



Portions of this book are based upon the author's previous publication of *The Galdrabók: An Icelandic Grimoire,* originally published in 1989 by Samuel Weiser, Inc., and by Rûna-Raven in 2005



**Library of Congress Cataloging-in-Publication Data**

Flowers, Stephen E., 1953–
[Galdrabók]
Icelandic magic : practical secrets of the northern grimoires / Stephen E. Flowers, Ph.D.
pages cm
Includes bibliographical references and index.
ISBN 978-1-62055-405-0 (pbk.) — ISBN 978-1-62055-406-7 (e-book)
1. Magic, Germanic—Handbooks, manuals, etc.—Early works to 1800. 2. Mythology, Germanic—Early works to 1800. 3. Iceland—Religion—Early works to 1800. I. Title.
BF1622.G3F56 2016
133.4'3094912—dc23

2015012309

Printed and bound in the United States by Versa Press, Inc.

10 9 8 7

Text design by Debbie Glogover and layout by Priscilla Baker
This book was typeset in Garamond Premier Pro with Goudy Old Style used as a display typeface

To send correspondence to the author of this book, mail a first-class letter to the author c/o Inner Traditions • Bear & Company, One Park Street, Rochester, VT 05767, and we will forward the communication or visit the author's website at **www.seekthemystery.com**.

# Contents

## Part Two
## Gray-Skin

## Notes to the Reader

### Abbreviations

| | |
|---|---|
| ch. | chapter |
| Ice. | Icelandic |
| Lat. | Latin |
| Lbs. | Landsbókasafn (= National Library of Iceland) |
| ON | Old Norse |
| PGmc. | Proto-Germanic |
| pl. | plural |
| sg. | singular |
| st. | stanza |

### Orthography

Old Norse and modern Icelandic feature several letters that are not found in the Roman alphabet: *þ*, which represents an unvoiced */th/* sound (sometimes transliterated as *th*), and *ð*, which represents a voiced */th/* sound (sometimes transliterated as *dh*).

### Foreign Words

Words appearing in parentheses or square brackets are Old Norse or Icelandic unless otherwise indicated. There are only slight variations in spelling between Old Norse and early modern Icelandic.

## *FOREWORD*

# Magic Manuals and Sorcerous Staves

By Michael Moynihan

Grimoires are magic manuals: handbooks for making and activating talismans, spells, and curses. A widespread phenomenon, they represent an ancient literary genre in the history of magic, witchcraft, and heretical religious practices. Countless examples have been found in Western, Middle Eastern, and Eastern cultures. Across the whole of Europe an especially robust grimoire tradition has existed for centuries and has recently been detailed in works by historians of folk belief such as Owen Davies and Claude Lecouteux.* America can even claim its own contribution to the genre: the early-nineteenth-century compendium of folk magic and medicine collected by John George Hohman under the curious title *Der lang verborgene Freund* (The Long-Lost Friend).† I suspect that contemporary witchcraft and occult practices such as the Gardnerian "Book

*See Davies, *Grimoires: A History of Magic Books;* Lecouteux, *The Book of Grimoires: The Secret Grammar of Magic* and *Dictionary of Ancient Magic Words and Spells: From Abraxas to Zoar*. Full citations for these works are provided in the bibliography at the back of this book.

†See Hohman, *The Long-Lost Friend: A 19th Century American Grimoire,* edited and annotated by Daniel Harms.

of Shadows" or the Crowleyan "Magickal Diary" are, at root, attempts to follow in the footsteps of—or reinvent—the older grimoire tradition, albeit in a largely subjective and ahistorical way. Countless other modern manifestations of grimoire-like texts could be cataloged in the same vein.

The word *grimoire* as we use it today derives from a borrowing of the Old French term *gram(m)aire.* This originally referred to a book written in Latin but soon came to denote a book of magic: the shift in meaning may have come about because the European grimoires were typically filled with (often garbled) Latin, not to mention smatterings of Greek and other foreign words and phrases. The word *grimoire* has the same origin as *grammar,* and a certain overlap can still be seen between them, at least in the sense of a book filled with prescriptions for proper communication, using the medium of letters and written symbols (one should not forget that both terms ultimately derive from the Greek *gramma,* "written letter, character"). In the case of a grimoire, that communication is with the hidden forces of the universe, both demonic and divine.

In addition to the inclusion of magical words from foreign languages, a common feature of many grimoires is the use of strange alphabets, ciphers, and signs to represent specific deities, demons, or other hidden forces. While many of these symbols were copied and recopied, and thereby came to constitute an inherited visual vocabulary, there was also room for the individual magician to adapt and modify such material according to personal knowledge, and even to create new symbols when needed. The symbols became further codified when grimoires began to be mechanically printed and sold clandestinely in the form of chapbooks, but this did not wipe out the older tradition in which individuals copied down their own grimoires by hand or wrote them out for others. Many such examples have been found, all the way up into the early twentieth century. As personal expressions, no two are exactly alike.

A thriving grimoire tradition has existed in Scandinavian countries since the late Middle Ages, with many surviving examples now preserved in manuscript archives. In Norway they are called "black books" (*svartebøker*); in Sweden, "black art books" (*svartkonstböcker*) or "sorcery books" (*trolldomsböcker*); and in Iceland, "magic books" (*galdrabækur*). The Icelandic texts are particularly distinguished, for a *galdrabók* typically exhibits a striking visual element in the often elaborate *galdrastafir* (magic staves) that decorate its pages and which are a central component to many of the spells. While the use of symbols and graphic "signatures" was a well-established aspect of the continental grimoire tradition, the Icelanders developed their variety of magic staves to a unique art. And whereas the continental grimoires tend to only make reference to Greco-Mediterranean and Judeo-Christian deities and demons, the Icelandic grimoires preserve remarkable vestiges of Germanic heathen folklore. Grimoires even played a significant role in Icelandic religious history, as Magnús Rafnsson explains: "Almost a third of the known witchcraft trials in Iceland revolve around magical staves and signs, grimoires, and pages with occult writings. In some cases the accused owned one or more grimoires, in a few instances signs and sigils had been written on other objects, sometimes pieces of oak, gills, or even boats."*

More than a quarter-century ago, Stephen Flowers published *The Galdrabók: An Icelandic Grimoire,* an annotated translation of the most remarkable extant Icelandic grimoire, dated to the late sixteenth century. At the time his book appeared, material on the late medieval and early modern Icelandic magical traditions and folk practices was quite difficult to come by, particularly in the English-speaking world. Stephen's book even sold briskly in Iceland—the inhabitants of that island have an abiding interest in their own past and culture—and several years later, in 1992, the first scholarly modern Icelandic study of the *Galdrabók* was published by Matthías Viðar Sæmundsson.

In recent years a number of other Icelandic magical manuscripts and books have been reproduced and translated in modern editions. A good deal of this renaissance of curiosity about Icelandic folk magic has been fueled by the creation of Strandagaldur, a small museum dedicated to the history of Icelandic magic and witchcraft. Established at the turn

---

*Rafnsson, *Angurgapi: The Witch-Hunts in Iceland,* 53.

of the millennium, Strandagaldur is fittingly located at Hólmavík in the remote Strandir region of the northwest fjords—an area already notorious as a home to sorcerers and outlaws in the medieval saga literature. The museum features permanent and temporary exhibits on various aspects of Icelandic folklore and history, specifically in relation to magical practices and witchcraft.

In rural areas Scandinavian black books were still being copied—and presumably used—into the early twentieth century. Now and then they are rediscovered, such as when Mary Rustad found two such black books in the 1970s while rummaging in the attic of her ancestors' farm in Elverum, Norway. Originally dating from 1790–1820, the books have been republished in a facsimile edition and English translation. Of even more interest in the present context is an Icelandic grimoire called *Rún*—literally, "rune," but the word also has a more abstract meaning of "secret or hidden lore"—written or copied in 1928 and containing a considerable number of *galdrastafir* along with a veritable host of encryption alphabets. This has recently been published in high-quality facsimile by the Strandagaldur museum.

Unlike the aforementioned editions, the present book is not a reproduction of a historical grimoire per se, although it is informed by a number of such texts and incorporates genuine traditional material for the majority of its content. It is rather a handbook and how-to manual for those who wish to begin experimenting within this tradition themselves. The first half of the book (largely based upon the introductory portion of Stephen's earlier study, *The Galdrabók*) gives an overview of Icelandic magic in its historical and literary context, thus enabling a deeper understanding of the roots of the Icelandic *galdrabækur* culture. The most famous legends surrounding historical Icelandic sorcerers and their personal grimoires are also translated here. The first part of the book concludes with two chapters that offer an insightful methodology (including preparation, ritual, and usage) for the creation of one's own *galdrastafir*. The second part of the book offers a basic set of spells that make up a working *galdrabók*. In addition to those spells and staves derived from original Icelandic sources, several new ones have been created—and tested for efficacy—by the author. Once grounded in the fundamentals of the tradition, the owner of the book is encouraged to continue actively experimenting on his or her own.

Stephen Flowers is the perfect person to write a primer on Icelandic magic. For more than half a century he has been studying ancient Germanic culture and religion, as well as Old Norse and Icelandic language, literature, and mythology. He is scientifically trained in runology and also founded the Rune-Gild, an initiatory organization dedicated to traditionally informed esoteric work with the runes. He has likewise immersed himself in the history of Western magic, in particular that of heretical personalities and movements. His teachers and mentors in these subjects were some of the greatest scholars in their respective fields. In August of 1995 he traveled to Iceland to a retreat on the Snæfellsnes peninsula, where he gave a series of talks and workshops about the *galdrastafir* and related aspects of Icelandic magic. He was able to do some of this in Icelandic and gave a general lecture in Icelandic as well—no small feat, given the complexities of the language.

Starting in the mid-1980s, upon the completion of his Ph.D., Stephen began publishing books of a spiritual nature under his pen name, Edred Thorsson. These dealt with Germanic religion and runology from a practical standpoint, and his personal involvement in such areas would prove highly influential in the years that followed. In contrast to the Edred Thorsson titles, Stephen wrote and published several books of a more scholarly nature—the original edition of *The Galdrabók* among them—under his given name. For decades he kept up this distinction between his scientific and his spiritual works. With *Icelandic Magic,* however, readers will find a book published under his birth name that is deeply invested with scholarship but which also represents a working manual for the practitioner. Stephen tells me that, at this stage of his career, maintaining the public distinction between the two sides of his work—the scholarly and the esoteric, the theoretical and the practical—no longer matters.

In the rich corpus of Icelandic legends and folktales, certain notorious grimoires take on a life and history of their own. At the very least, a grimoire should reflect the soul of its creator or owner. The creation of an Icelandic *galdrabók* has always been an art form, but one which—like the best art—continually exerts its magic in the real world, beyond the two-dimensions of parchment, paper, or canvas. *Icelandic Magic* should not be thumbed through and tucked away in a research library or confined to a curiosity cabinet. This manual is meant to be used.

A new wave of interest in the folkways of our ancestors is under way. Much old lore, preserved in all manner of hidden places, has been rediscovered, collected, and brought back out into the light of day. But one need not remain a passive consumer of the past. A new generation of researchers and practitioners is already trying to unlock and reactivate the mysteries of the *galdrabækur* and *galdrastafir.** And now you, the reader of this book, can also become the *writer* and try your hand at stirring the sorcerous staves to life, sending them out into the wide world to work their magic.

MICHAEL MOYNIHAN is an author, translator, editor, and musician. His nonfiction book *Lords of Chaos* (cowritten with Didrik Søderlind; revised edition: Feral House, 2003), an underground bestseller translated into nine languages, is now the basis for a feature film production. He has contributed to scholarly encyclopedias and topical anthologies, and coedits (with Joshua Buckley) the journal *TYR: Myth—Culture—Tradition.* He recently collaborated on *American Grotesque,* the first monograph of work by William Mortensen (1897–1965), an unsung early-twentieth-century pioneer of grotesque and occult photography, along with a new edition of Mortensen's aesthetic handbook, *The Command to*

*In Iceland, the work of Magnús Rafnsson, produced in collaboration with the Strandagaldur museum, is of particular note. Christopher Smith has written an excellent study, *Icelandic Magic: Aims, Tools and Techniques of the Icelandic Sorcerers*, and Justin Foster has recently made available a translation of the nineteenth-century Huld manuscript, a stunning document that contains many examples of *galdrastafir.*

*Look* (both published by Feral House, 2014). As a translator his work includes the annotated English edition of *Barbarian Rites: The Spiritual World of the Vikings and the Germanic Tribes* by Hans-Peter Hasenfratz, Ph.D. (Inner Traditions, 2011). Together with his wife, Annabel Lee, he runs Dominion Press, a small press that has produced limited-edition volumes by Hans Bellmer, Julius Evola, Stephen E. Flowers, Joscelyn Godwin, and John Michell.

# Preface

This is a practical grammar of the kind of magic practiced in Iceland from the Middle Ages forward. From a theoretical standpoint it is partially based on the pagan practices that preceded the coming of Christianity, but as it stands in its grand synthetic form it is a mixture of various kinds of magic. This mixture is unique to Iceland. Many of its techniques can easily be applied by practitioners within various traditions. As a synthesis of disparate traditions it is a good model for the individual magician of today. We are lucky that so much magical material was recorded by Icelanders throughout history and that so many of the books in which their records were kept have survived. One of the things that makes this kind of literature so worthy of our attention is the fact that it represents part of a continuing tradition and transmission of ideas from the pre-Christian age right up until the twentieth century. The tradition of recording magical spells in books went on in secret in Iceland on a scale that is only revealed by the number of surviving manuscripts in the *Landsbókasafn,* the National Library in Reykjavík.

Medieval books of magic were often called "grimoires," a word derived from the French *grammaire.* These books provided principles from which magicians could create their own magical operations. This is the main intent of this book as well. Much of the practical material presented here is taken directly from actual Icelandic sources.

Principal among these is the famous book that has come to be called the *Galdrabók* (book of magic), which is one of the earliest and most elaborate examples of an Icelandic grimoire text that has been preserved. Additional historical examples are drawn from various other Icelandic books of magic, as well as from a few personal experiments.

STEPHEN E. FLOWERS,
WOODHARROW INSTITUTE FOR
INDO-EUROPEAN STUDIES

# *INTRODUCTION*
# A Magical Text

The book you hold in your hands is an entirely pragmatic and practical work of magic. It is not primarily intended to be a historical study or a scientific study of Icelandic magic. This text is a magical one, and the book itself is a magical object. In this work are revealed some of the most powerful forms of magic known from the annals of the Icelandic "black books." Various secrets of these books are revealed here, and the book itself contains many more mysteries to be unlocked. When these mysteries, or unknown aspects, are discovered and the riddles unraveled, a rush of magical power will be made available to you. This is why the mysteries are present—not so much to hide things from you as to provide you with power. As an owner of this book, you have been chosen by fate, or *örløg,* to make use of its magical power. Use it wisely.

Although this is not *primarily* a historical study, the would-be practitioner of galdor-sign magic should be aware of the history of this form of magic and the cultural context in which it originated.

Built into many of the spells of the book are certain mysteries or secrets—words written in runes—for example. These mysterious elements suggest that the practitioner learn the meaning of these elements and that there is something about the information that should remain hidden or secret. If something is deliberately kept secret, this charges the object of secrecy with additional powers not attainable in any other fashion. The fact that there are so few real secrets in the world today leads to the feeling that there is little magical power in the world either.

This is a complete workbook. Part 1 of the book provides the contextual background for the tradition itself. It contains enough history for you to know about the heritage you are working with, and it contains historical examples of the practice of Icelandic magic. Based on a solid historical foundation, it demonstrates to you how you can become creative within the system in a traditional way. The final chapter of part 1 describes the basic procedures for both the ancient and modern practice of galdor-stave magic. Part 2 of the book, which is titled Gray-Skin, constitutes a working set of actual galdor-magic spells. The title alludes to the Gráskinna, a semi-mythical grimoire that is said to have been used by several legendary Icelandic magicians of the past. In the Gray-Skin section of the present book you will find a selection of traditional spells (translated from the *Galdrabók* and other manuscripts) along with several new spells that have been composed based on the principles of the tradition. A number of pages have been left blank for you at the back of this book so you can add your own records of successful magical workings within the system. When these are added you will have created another true book of magic, unique to yourself.

PART ONE

# *Historical Background and Basics of Magical Practice*

# Historical Context

In the distant past *galdrabækur* (magic books, sing. *galdrabók*), also known as "black books," were thought to possess their own special and innate power. Their physical existence was a threat to the status quo of the universe—as is the book you now possess. This is why they were hunted down and destroyed as if they were dangerous beasts in Iceland during the early modern period. However, this did not stop the stalwart galdor men of the northern Atlantic. Such books of magic continued to be compiled and hidden away by men (and a few women) in a private and secret way right up until the middle of the twentieth century. Some of these books survived and eventually found their way into the National Library of Iceland. But for every one that survived there must have been a hundred that did not.

In and of itself, a galdor book is a magical object and the chief icon of this kind of magic. What you now possess is also a genuine book of magic and should be treated with reverence to ensure that it maintains its magical essence. It is also essential for you to keep the power level of the book up by adding your own *galdrastafir* (galdor staves or signs) to the text as you master the inner language and grammar of the staves. This will make your book what every *galdrabók* is supposed to be: a unique expression of the magician who is the owner of the book.

Much has rightly been made of the uniqueness of the traditions of Icelandic magic—how it is fundamentally different from the type of magic that might have been imported from the continent of Europe in the Middle Ages. Nevertheless, certain features from the South were certainly incorporated in the new Icelandic synthesis of magical tradition. This new synthesis brought together elements of ancient Germanic magic, classic medieval magic (largely derived from the Mediterranean region), and combined these with an innovative and pragmatic magical technology belonging to Iceland.

To establish a context for the magic practiced in the Icelandic magical books that began being set down in the early 1500s, we must look at the various stages of religious and cultural development in Iceland. There are three such periods: the Heathen Age, the Catholic Age, and the Protestant Reformation Age.

Iceland was first settled in the latter decades of the ninth century, mainly by Norwegians (along with their Celtic thralls). These Norwegians sought political and religious freedom from the monarchical onslaught of King Haraldr *Hárfagra* (Harald Fairhair). Under the political influence of already Christianized Europe, the still-pagan Haraldr had set about to conquer all of Norway and govern it as a Christian-style monarchy.

Icelanders formed a social order deeply rooted in their Scandinavian heritage. This was a sort of representative or republican aristocracy. Iceland never had a king. The island was governed by the local priest-chieftains (ON *goðar,* sing. *goði*), who would meet once a year at the *Althing* (great assembly), or parliament. There legal cases were settled, and other affairs of state were conducted. This form of government exercised a minimum of central authority. Courts could decide capital cases but in fact had no ability to execute any sentences. The actual punishment was left up to the kinsmen of the wronged party. For example, those who had committed manslaughter would be "outlawed." This means that they would be declared to be outside the protection of the law, and thus they could be killed without legal repercussions to the avengers. Another main feature of Germanic law was the idea that the wronged party was the one entitled to compensation by the criminal. In other words, the "state" did not profit from crime. A monetary value was set for almost every sort of crime. This meant that a man might be able to satisfy the wronged party with a monetary payment instead of being outlawed. In the case of murder, the penalty was called *manngjöld,* literally meaning "man-payment" (the equivalent term in Old English is *weregild*). Each *goði* held an authority (ON *goðorð,* which means "authority as a *goði*") that approximately corresponded to a district in the country. The authority in question was thought to be *owned* by the *goði* as a form of property and could be sold, inherited, or subdivided.

At first the Icelanders practiced the religion they brought with them from Scandinavia—an age-old polytheistic Germanic heathenism. This is a religion that allowed for much individual freedom, and such views influenced the original form of the Icelandic system of state government. One man may have worshipped Óðinn (Odin); another, Þórr (Thor); another, Freyja (Freya); and yet another may have "believed in his own might and main." It is also true that there were a number of Christians among the Celtic thralls brought to Iceland from Ireland and the islands of the North Atlantic, and a few of their masters even converted. However, these conversions did not survive to the next generation in those families. But it is important to keep in mind that the first Icelanders tolerated these differences.

By the end of the first millennium, most of Iceland's main trading partners—Ireland, England, Norway, and Denmark—had nominally been Christianized. In Iceland, Christianity was formally accepted as the official religion on the basis of a vote at the Althing in the year 1000. This occurred under a variety of social, economic, and religious pressures, although deep religious belief does not seem to have played a great role.

The reception of Christianity by the Icelanders was in many ways formalistic, marked by little conviction even on the part of those who voted to accept it. Public sacrifices to the Germanic gods were outlawed, but private practices of the traditional faith were allowed to continue. These included the eating of horseflesh and the exposure of unwanted or deformed infants. Conversion to Roman Catholicism was marked by a lengthy and gradual transition period. This process lasted for several generations. There was also an undiminished interest on the part of Icelanders in their own native traditions. In the earliest phase of this historical period many of the *goðar* just had themselves ordained as Christian priests without any further education or training. Others lent their religious duties to relatives. This was because the traditional synthesis of "religious" and "secular" authority seemed un-Christian. There were also officials known as *leiguprestar* (hired priests) who were bound to a chieftain like thralls.

For the first thirty years of this period Iceland would have remained largely heathen in its practice of religion and magic, as there was no one there to teach them differently. Following this time there was a period referred to as the *Friðaröld,* the Age of Peace, from 1030 to 1118. During the Age of Peace feuding subsided and a new culture began to take hold as individual Icelanders started to observe the tenets of the new religion. This could also be called a period of mixed faith, as Christianity actually began to gain some foothold in the culture. For this it was necessary for Icelandic clerics and scholars to travel abroad to learn of the new faith, and then schools began to be established in Iceland itself. In the latter part of this period the Icelandic language began to be used to record histories, sagas, and poetry.

A general love of written literature developed in the country. This led some men to join the clergy to be educated abroad and others to enter monasteries out of a love of learning. Some wealthy men set up schools on their private estates. There they worked as scholars and teachers. These traditions of learning were in fact deeply rooted in the pagan age, in which oral tradition was just as lovingly preserved. It should be recalled that Iceland was settled largely by the culturally conservative aristocracy of Norway. This led to an unusually high level of interest in national intellectual traditions, even in later times. Today it is reported that Iceland has the highest literacy rate and the highest per capita book-publishing rate in the world.

These developments do not seem to have appreciably changed the nature of the church or clergy in Iceland. There was always a vigorous secular element in the Icelandic church and a strain of cultural conservatism. All this fostered the preservation and continuation of national traditions in statecraft, religion, and literary culture. It is also important to note that those Icelanders who joined the church and the monasteries during this time were not forced to reject worldly pleasures for ascetic lives of strict piety. The rule of celibacy was never enforced in the Icelandic priesthood. Priests could not marry according to church law, but this fact simply left the door open for the continuity of the age-old practice of polygamy, or "multiconcubinage." In most respects the old ways just carried on in new forms.

The Age of Peace began to disintegrate in a period of civil strife that began around 1118. The old behaviors of feuding, blood vengeance, and similar patterns began to reemerge, and to this were added elements of political conspiracy and intrigue involving foreign powers and the offices of the church. Although aspects of such civil unrest would continue for centuries, in 1262 the situation was sharply curtailed by the forceful intervention of the Norwegian king. The era of Norwegian dominance lasted until 1397, when Norway was absorbed by the Kingdom of Denmark in the Kalmar Union. Thus began the long period of Danish domination, which would last for centuries. In 1944, during the time when the Danes found themselves rather distracted while under Nazi occupation (1940–1945), Iceland was able to once again establish its complete independence.

In spite of the domestic strife and foreign exploitation endured by the Icelanders between the end of the Age of Peace and the beginning of Danish domination, this period was nevertheless a sort of golden age of Icelandic culture and literature. It was at this time that the poems of the *Poetic Edda* were committed to parchment, when Snorri Sturluson wrote the *Prose Edda* (1222), and when most of the great sagas were compiled. It seems that Icelanders had become comfortable with their "National Catholicism," which had allowed indigenous traditions to survive and native "saints" (some official, some not) to be revered.

The Protestant Reformation itself began with Martin Luther in Germany in 1517. It rapidly spread throughout northern Europe. It was there that secular authorities, the kings and princes, had long harbored cultural animosities toward the centuries-long domination of Rome. In 1536 the Reformation was officially accepted in Denmark. This meant that Iceland, as a possession of the Danish crown, was also destined to follow that course. Because Iceland continued to be isolated, and due to its intrinsic conservatism, the Reformation did not come easily to the island.

There were two sources for the Reformation in Iceland: the foreign forces of the Dano-Norwegian crown and the domestic clerics who had become convinced of Luther's doctrines. This often occurred when they were studying abroad in Denmark or Germany. One of the reasons the crowned heads of northern Europe found Protestantism so attractive is that it allowed the kings to nationalize—and, in effect, confiscate—the wealth and properties of the Catholic Church in their countries. On the other hand, resistance to the Reformation came mostly from the conservative populace and, of course, from the Catholic clergy still loyal to Rome. From 1536 to 1550 there existed what amounted to a low-intensity war in Iceland. The forces of Protestantism, which is to say the crown, finally won with the execution of Bishop Jón Árason in 1550. But this only marked the beginning of any real Reformation at the popular level. Certainly it would take a full century, until around 1650, before Protestantism could be considered to have been fully accepted by the population at large. Catholicism itself was receding into the past.

It was within the cultural mixture of the heathen heritage and the recent Catholic past that the magic contained in various Icelandic *galdrabækur* was first practiced. But it was during this period of religious change—and, ultimately, of religious persecution—that the magical work was actually committed to parchment and paper.

This time of "popular Reformation" was marked by increasing economic exploitation and political domination by the Danes. In 1602,

Denmark established a trade monopoly over the country, which meant that Icelandic merchants could no longer trade freely with other countries. The resulting period of economic hardship is one that is often reflected in the folktales of the time. Powerful Danish tradesmen and the Protestant churchmen (who were virtual agents of the Danish crown) ruthlessly exploited and oppressed the people. A full quarter of the tithe paid to the church and the fines imposed by the courts went directly to the king of Denmark. The laws of the country were also altered to impose the death penalty for moral crimes such as heresy and adultery. At first the charge of heresy was mainly aimed against those thought to practice Catholicism in secret, but the net would eventually be expanded to include "witchcraft." As in other Protestant countries of the time, defendants who were convicted of such crimes had to forfeit some or all of their personal estate to the king. In certain areas this process led to the practice of industrial and entrepreneurial "witch hunting," in which the estate of the executed witch would be divided three ways between the state, the judge, and the "witch finder." Although similar procedures were established in Iceland, it must be said that the situation there never escalated to the level of genocidal executions such as took place in seventeenth-century Germany.

Throughout the 1600s Iceland spiraled downward into economic and political decay. But the age was not without its benefits, for the scholarly humanism that developed throughout Scandinavia gave rise to a concerted effort by antiquarians to save the Icelandic literary heritage. However, like the economic wealth of the nation, its cultural treasures were also siphoned off to Copenhagen. Ironically, these antiquities were probably actually saved by the Danish scholars from the material ravages wreaked by Danish tradesmen. Many manuscripts that remained uncollected were in fact eaten by starving Icelanders, or, for want of other materials, were used to make shoes or clothing! In the decades following Iceland's independence in 1944, most of the important manuscripts that had been preserved in Denmark were repatriated back to the island.

# History of Magic in Iceland

There is an unusually large amount of information about many aspects of the practice of magic by the Icelanders that amounts to much more than any other non-Greco-Roman European people. The Icelanders left behind a clear record of their magical beliefs and practices and have also given us some clear ideas about the contexts in which this magic was practiced. Not only do we have original pagan sources (in the *Poetic Edda* and skaldic poetry) but also some clear reflections of pre-Christian practices set down in saga literature. The sagas are prose works of literature. Written down for the most part between 1120 and 1400, these semi-historical tales usually reflect events and beliefs of the Viking Age (about 800–1100).

## THE PRE-CHRISTIAN AGE

Icelandic sagas sometimes feature the working of magic and give us vivid pictures of the lives of several magicians. The most famous of these is *Egil's Saga*. This is essentially a biography of Egill Skallagrímsson (910–990), an Icelandic skaldic poet, runic magician, and follower of the god Óðinn. From later periods we have the rare finds of actual manuals of magic. Along with runic inscriptions, legal records, and other documents, these works provide correlations to the "literary" material and fill in some of the gaps left by the sagas and poems.

As with other aspects of Icelandic history, the earliest phases can be divided into the pre-Christian and Catholic periods. The later Reformation or Protestant period changed the picture considerably. It was during the Protestant Age that most of the books of magic were created, but in order to make any headway in comprehending the magical worldview of these magicians it is also necessary to understand the cosmos of the Germanic heathen past.

As should be clear from the previous discussion of the history and character of the church during the Catholic period, the mixture of pagan and Christian elements prevalent in Icelandic culture shows how and why we are able to use documents actually written down in the Catholic period as somewhat reliable sources for the heathen practice of magic. As far as magic is concerned, this was really more an age of synthesis than a radical departure from the past, and the same holds true for other aspects of the older culture.

The accounts we have make it clear that in the later pagan age there seem to have been two kinds of magic being practiced: *galdr* (Modern Icelandic spelling: *galdur*) and *seiðr* (Modern Icelandic spelling: *seiður*). These appear to have taken on some moral connotations—the *galdr* form being more "honorable" and the *seiðr* form often considered "shameful" or "womanish"—although originally there were probably only certain technical (and perhaps social) distinctions between the two. The Old Norse word *galdr* is derived from the verb *gala,* "to crow, chant," and is therefore marked by the use of the incantational formula that is spoken or sung, and perhaps also carved in runes. The original meaning of *seiðr* may also have something to do with vocal performance (i.e., singing or chanting), although the exact original meaning of the word remains unclear. It is derived from the verb *síða,* "to enchant." One thing is certain, however: contrary to the claims of some modern authors, the word has nothing to do with "boiling" or "seething."

There are clear procedural and psychological distinctions between these two magical techniques. The practice of *galdr* is more analytical, conscious, willed, and ego oriented, whereas *seiðr* is more intuitive and synthetic. Typical of the *galdr* technique is the assumption of a "magical persona," or alter ego, for working the will. In *seiðr,* by contrast, a trance state is induced in which ego-consciousness is temporarily obliterated. It has also sometimes been said that *seiðr* is closer to what is commonly thought of as "shamanic" practice. It should also be pointed out that although these are two real tendencies in Icelandic pagan magic, the *moral* distinction appears to be a later development. Óðinn is called the "father" of *galdr* (ON *Galdrafõðr*) and its natural master, but it is also reported that he learned the arts of *seiðr* from the Vanic goddess Freyja.

One traditional field of Germanic magic from which the *galdur* of our texts inherits many of its methods is that of "rune magic." The runes (Ice. *rúnar* or *rúnir*) form a writing system used by the Germanic peoples from perhaps as early as 200 BCE. The use of runes survived into the early nineteenth century in some remote areas of Scandinavia. Such runes, or rune staves (Ice. *rúnstafir*) as they were often called, were at first used for non-profane purposes. By around 1000 CE they began to be used increasingly for ordinary communication. The word *rún* in Icelandic signifies not only one of the "staves," or signs, used in writing, but also the idea of a "mystery," "secret," or "body of secret lore." This idea of "secret lore"—which in fact reflects the original sense of the word *rún*—was then transferred to the phonetic signs (writing) that made communication over time and space possible.

Just before the inception of the Viking Age, the last pagan recodification of the runes took place. It was out of this time period that many of the pre-Christian aspects of magical practice found in the historical books of Icelandic magic seem to have grown. As in earlier times, each rune had a name as well as its phonetic value (usually corresponding to the first sound in its name). There were also interpretative poetic stanzas connected to each rune. These are of great interest to us as they were recorded in Iceland and Norway in the

1400s and 1500s, a time period that is actually quite close to when our earliest texts of galdor magic were composed. We can be fairly certain, therefore, that the *galdramenn* (magicians) had some detailed knowledge of the esoteric lore of pagan runology. Many of them were certainly literate in runes. The system of the Viking Age runes, as it would have been known to the Icelanders, is shown in table 2 (see pages 106–7).

Several things can be learned directly from this table about the significance of what we encounter in the spells discovered in historical books of magic. The number 16 is often found underlying the composition of the stave forms in the spells. Most often these are not actual rune staves; rather they tend to be stylized magical letters or abstract symbols. However, they do reflect the formulaic significance of the number 16, which is the total number of runes in the Viking Age rune row. Additionally, the rune names occur in the spells themselves, where they apparently signify the corresponding runes. Certain rune names, such as *hagall* (hail), also show up in the technical names of the special "magical signs" (Ice. *galdrastafir*) themselves.

In pre-Christian times rune magicians were usually well-known and honored members of society. In the Northern tradition, runelore had been the preserve of members of an established social order interested in intellectual or spiritual pursuits. Most commonly these men were followers of the god Óðinn, the Germanic god of magic, ecstasy, poetry, and death. Historically, men were more often engaged in rune magic than were women—a social phenomenon that is reflected in the later statistics concerning witchcraft trials in Iceland. These statistics show that men were more likely to be accused of practicing witchcraft than were women.

In pagan times the technique of rune magic consisted of three main procedural steps, as follows:

1. carving the staves into an object
2. coloring with blood (or dye)

3. speaking a vocal formula over the staves to load them with magical power

The basic components of this direct technique, which is not dependent on any intervention by gods or demons, will later be continued in the historical *galdrabækur.* This direct mode of operation clearly shows the continuation of a practice from early Germanic times right up to the modern age. It must also be noted that the technique is generally thought to have to be performed by a qualified rune magician. This is true of most traditional forms of magic.

Old Icelandic literature contains some examples of this kind of magic. One of the most interesting examples is found in the *Poetic Edda* in the poem called, alternately, "För Skírnis" or the "Skírnismál" (st. 36). This poem dates from the early tenth century. In it the messenger of the god Freyr, who is named Skírnir, is trying to force the beautiful giantess to love his lord, Freyr. Skírnir threatens her with a curse.

| | |
|---|---|
| *Þurs ríst ek þér* | *A thurs-rune I carve for you,* |
| *ok þría stafi* | *and three staves (they are)—* |
| *ergi ok œði* | *wantonness and frenzy* |
| *ok óþola;* | *and torment;* |
| *svá ek þat af ríst* | *I shall scrape it off* |
| *sem ek þat á reist,* | *as I scratched it on,* |
| *ef gøraz þarfar þess.* | *if it becomes necessary.* |

The basic stance of the rune magician that we see here, as well as the technical aspects such as the enumeration of the staves and the actual style of the incantation, will be likewise found in the practical workings that appear centuries later in Icelandic books of magic.

One other famous example that clearly shows rune-magic techniques is found in *Egil's Saga* (ch. 44). Here we see Egill detecting poison that had been put in his drinking horn:

Egill drew out his knife and stabbed the palm of his hand. He took the horn, carved runes on it, and rubbed blood on them. He said:

*I carve a rune on the horn*
*I redden the spell in blood*
*these words I choose for the horn . . .*

The horn burst asunder, and the drink went down into the straw.*

In addition to rune magic, and sometimes combined with it, we find workings used in pre-Christian times that make use of certain magically potent natural substances. In fact there was a whole magical classification system of sacred woods only partially reflected in the *galdrabækur.* It appears that woods of various trees played a special part in Germanic magical technology as well as its mythology. The cosmos is said to be formed around the framework of a tree called *Yggdrasill.* In the "Völuspá" (sts. 17–18) humankind is shown to have been shaped by a threefold hypostasis of Óðinn-Hœnir-Lóðurr from trees: the man from ash and the woman from elm.

Blood is another substance of extreme importance. Runes were often reddened with it, and it was generally known to have intrinsic magical powers, especially when the blood was that of the magician himself. In many pre-Christian sacrificial rites the blood of the animal was sprinkled onto the altar, temple walls, and even the gathered worshippers. Everything was thought to be hallowed by this contact. Actually, the etymology of the English verb "to bless" reflects this heathen practice. The word is derived from the Proto-Germanic form *blōðisōjan* ("to hallow with blood" from PGmc. *blōðam,* "blood").

Herbal substances were also widely used in pre-Christian magical practice. Some of the most powerful of these were species of leek (Ice. *laukur*), the name of which commonly occurs as a magical runic formula even as early as 450 CE. Several herbs also bear the names of

*See Pálsson and Edwards, trans., *Egil's Saga,* 101.

Norse gods or goddesses; for example, Icelandic *Friggjargras* ("Frigg's herb")* and *Baldursbrá* ("Baldur's brow").†

## CATHOLIC PERIOD

As will be remembered from our discussion of the politico-religious history of Iceland, a peculiar kind of Catholic Church existed in Iceland from 1000 to the middle of the 1500s. In all facets of life this represented a period of religious syncretism in which elements of the ancient native heritage and the new foreign religion were being blended together. This is the period just prior to the time when the Icelandic books of magic began to be composed.

Pagan elements would naturally tend to be diminished over time, both as new material was introduced and as knowledge of the technical aspects of the pagan tradition began to fade through neglect and lack of old established support. Nevertheless, the old material and techniques continued in a real way for many generations. In many respects, however, this is a "dark age" for our knowledge of the actual practice of magic in Iceland. This is because the works composed at this time tended to depict earlier Viking Age practices, and we have no actual *galdrabækur* from the period itself.

There are a number of runic inscriptions from Scandinavia that help fill in the gap in our knowledge of the time; for example, the magical formulas found in Scandinavia from this period, which make use of (often defective) Latin formulas executed in the runic alphabet. This shows the blending of the Christian and pre-Christian cultures. The fact that the Latin is often riddled with grammatical errors

---

*Older sources identify this as *Orchis odoratissima, Satyrium albidium,* or even as the mandrake (a plant that does not grow in Iceland); modern research associates the name with the northern green orchid, *Platanthera hyperborea.*

†This herb is identified in older sources as *Cotula foetida, Pyrethrum inodorum,* or perhaps eye-bright (*Euphrasia* sp.) but in modern research as an aster, the sea mayweed (*Tripleurospermum maritimum*, syn. *Matricaria maritimum*).

demonstrates that these inscriptions were probably executed by laymen or young students. However, a few inscriptions are grammatically flawless, which shows that some members of the well-educated clergy also indulged in these arts. On the one hand, the fact that the formula is in Latin demonstrates the mythic dominance of Christian symbolism in the magician's world, but the fact that the inscription is executed in runes also shows that the old runic symbolism provided something to the inscription that the Latin alphabet was thought to lack.

A medieval rune stick found in Bergen reads:

**Fig. 2.1. maria perperit cristum, elisabet perperit iohannem baptisam in illarum ueneracione sis absolutaøcsi inkalue dominuste uacat adlu[cem]**

**Maria perperit Christum, Elisabeth perperit Iohannem Baptistam. In illarum veneratione sis absoluta! Exi, incolea! Dominus te vocat ad lucem!**

"Mary gave birth to Christ, Elizabeth gave birth to John the Baptist; in their veneration be absolved. Come out child, with hair! The Lord calls you to light!"

This is a Christian magical formula to allow for easy childbirth. It was believed that a child born with hair would be healthy.

Based on what we see in later material, it is possible to speculate that many features of the pagan tradition were kept alive for a long time but that eventually these were blended together with elements from the Christian medieval tradition that had come to the North during the long Christianization process. It must, however, be understood that practicing magic in the first place was considered by orthodox Christian dogmas to be heretical and even diabolical in and of itself. This may explain why there appears to have been an active, explicit merger between the old gods and the demons of hell, and even why demonic entities can appear in spells next to apparently orthodox religious figures such as Raphael or the Savior.

Christian influence on the tradition was most clearly seen in new elements introduced into the formulas. These include personalities from Judeo-Christian mythology such as Solomon, Jesus, and Mary. In addition to these figures, certain formulas were also incorporated during this period: the invocation of the Trinity, (Latin) formulas of benediction peculiar to the Catholic Church, the "Our Father" in Latin, and so on. Other elements, such as Judeo-Gnostic formulas (for example, Jehovah Sebaoth [Yahweh Tzabaoth], Tetragrammaton), must have come directly from magical books imported from the Continent. With regard to the actual methods of working magic, there was a shift in emphasis to the prayer formula in which the magician bids for the intercession of some supernatural entity on his behalf. Although this was known to some extent in the pre-Christian age, it had limited application. However, this form predominates as a mode of operation in the Judeo-Christian tradition.

We only have indirect information about magicians and magic of this period. Many texts were composed in this period, but they mostly harked back to the Heathen Age when magic came into play. Later folktales, for the most part collected in the 1700s and 1800s, report on one famous magician of this early age: Sæmundur Sigfússon the Wise (1056–1133). He was the *goði* (priest-chieftain) of Oddi. He is reputed to have been the most learned man of his time, but all of his writings are now lost. His fame was such even into modern times that the collection of poetry that came to be known as the *Poetic Edda* (or *Elder Edda*) was originally ascribed to him and called the *Sæmundar Edda*. Furthermore, he was said to have acquired a great deal of magical knowledge as a captive of the "Black School of Satan." This legend most likely stems from the fact that he was one of the first Icelanders to study Latin and theology on the Continent. Despite the supposed origin of his magical knowledge, Sæmundur had the reputation of being a "good" magician. The designation of "white" or "black" magic that the historical magicians acquired was due more to literary stereotyping and regional conflicts than to any historical or practical facts. Sæmundur's sister Halla also "practiced the old heathen lore," as one text describing her puts it, although the writer feels obliged to add that she was "nevertheless . . . a very religious woman."*

## PROTESTANT PERIOD

When Protestantism was introduced in Iceland beginning in about 1536, a radical new situation came into being. As learning decreased in quality for a time and persecutions of magic increased in intensity, elements of Icelandic magic already in place began to be increasingly admixed with elements from previously rejected paganism. The result of this was that the new Protestant establishment in some cases equated elements of Catholic practice with pagan lore.

As the Catholic period drew to a close, there lived two contemporary Icelandic magicians with very different reputations. One was Gottskálk Niklásson the Cruel (bishop of Hólar from 1497 to 1520), who had a reputation as an "evil" magician. He was said to be the compiler of the fabled Rauðskinna book of magic (further discussed in chapter 7). Gottskálk is otherwise well known in Icelandic history as a ruthless political schemer who conspired against secular political figures for his own benefit. This bad reputation is probably the real source of his image in the folk tradition. An approximate contemporary of Gottskálk was Hálfdanur Narfason (died 1568), vicar of Fell in Gottskálk's diocese of Hólar. Little is known of Hálfdanur's life, but there is a rich body of folktales concerning him. He appears as the legendary "white" counterpoint to the "black" bishop, Gottskálk.

Hálfdanur and Gottskálk stand at the gateway of transition between the Catholic and Reformation Ages in the history of Icelandic magic. Much later on in the Protestant period we again meet with a pair of

*See Simpson, *Legends of Icelandic Magicians,* 33.

strongly contrasted magicians: Eiríkur and Galdra-Loftur (Loftur the Magician). Eiríkur was a quiet and pious vicar who lived from 1637 to 1716. He is little known in history but shares with Sæmundur the reputation of being a practitioner of good magic, wholly derived from godly sources. This reputation was maintained despite the fact that he was not above practicing the most dreaded arts, such as necromancy, for "pedagogical purposes." Here I refer to one of the most telling anecdotes in the history of Icelandic magic—one that emphasizes the character, courage, and level of humor necessary to practice magic. This passage about Eiríkur testing two different boys who wanted to learn magic from him is translated in chapter 7.

This episode might be compared with part of the story about Galdra-Loftur in which he is supposed to have committed one of his most depraved acts—raising the *draugur* (ghost) of Bishop Gottskálk in an effort to take from his ghost the famous "black book," Rauðskinna, which had been buried with him. Not much is known of the historical Loftur other than that he was a scholar at the school of Hólar and he died in 1722. Galdra-Loftur is generally regarded as a kind of Icelandic Faust whose major "sin" lies in his insatiable desire for more knowledge and power. A translation of a passage from this folktale is presented in chapter 7 of this book as well.

As a result of Iceland's unique church organization during the Catholic period, together with the general isolation of the country from Continental affairs, the practice of magic was not officially persecuted or prosecuted during that time. The Inquisition became active on the Continent following Pope Innocent III's bull of 1199. This papal bull was primarily directed against what were believed to be organized heretics. Over time its authority widened to include sorcery, even when heresy was not involved, as was made clear in a bull by Pope Nicholas V in 1451. But even this failed to penetrate the dark mists of Thule. This phenomenon is probably in large part due to the fact that in Iceland it was clergymen themselves who were most actively engaged in sorcery!

Later on Protestants on the Continent were no less severe in dealing with witchcraft than the Catholic Inquisition had been, and in many cases they were more devastating since their focus on individuals and small groups tended to lead to indiscriminate persecutions. It was under the cover of the Reformation that real witchcraft persecutions came to Iceland. These persecutions never reached the genocidal levels known on the Continent, and especially in Germany, where hundreds of thousands were executed, but they are still historically significant for the small country of Iceland.

Some of the moral attitudes demonstrated by Icelanders toward magic being either good or evil may also go back to pagan sentiments. It would be a great mistake and error to assume that in pre-Christian times there was no such thing as "evil magic." Many of the spells of Óðinn reflected in the "Hávamál" are directed against evil sorcerers or witches. Clearly in pagan times the good was judged to be that which promoted the general welfare and defended humans, productive animals, crops, and so on. Evil was thought to be that which was destructive of good things or detrimental to the general welfare of the people, animals, or life in general. In Christian times, by contrast, the "good" was judged to be that which promoted the interests and dogmas of the church, and evil was anything set against these. The morality of the Icelandic magician was generally that of the pagan past, with little regard for the sources of the symbolism used.

The earliest trial for witchcraft in Iceland is recorded in 1554; the last such trial is recorded at the Althing of 1720. It must be said that records were poorly kept in this period, but it is estimated that during this time some 350 trials were held, although records for only 125 survive. Of these 125 accused persons, only 9 were women.* Obviously this is in stark contrast to the usual pattern of witchcraft accusations and suggests something of the demographics of actual magical practice in Iceland. It is also a general reflection of established Germanic tra-

*For statistics on Icelandic witchcraft trials, see Davíðsson, "Isländische Zauberzeichen und Zauberbücher," 150–51.

dition, where men were at least the equal of women when it came to the "occult" arts. Records exist for only twenty-six executions for witchcraft. These were mostly carried out by burning. Of the cases against female witches, only one woman was actually executed. Others who were convicted of this crime, but whose sentences were short of death, were flogged or outlawed. Outlawry meant that they were in effect banished from the country and sent into exile abroad.

Clearly the period of the most intensive witchcraft persecutions was between the first execution in 1625 and the last in 1685. However, it is worth noting that during this time Iceland suffered under a moral code of extremely harsh laws. These provided for capital punishment for a wide variety of crimes—murder, incest, adultery, theft—as well as witchcraft. Even finding rune staves carved on a stick or written on parchment was evidence sufficient to convict someone of witchcraft. This is a far cry from the saga age when great men knew the runes and the Althing could not impose the death penalty! It is also worth pointing out that although it was not necessarily the poorest or most ignorant people who were accused of sorcery, the rich and powerful or the scholarly (who were the chief practitioners, historically) were, for the most part, immune from prosecution.

In the period between 1550 and 1680 Iceland developed a form of magic that was practiced by members of the highest levels of its society. The fact that this synthesis survived as long as it did, however, is perhaps due to the relative lack of a strict set of socioeconomic and educational class distinctions in Iceland. Even today Icelanders are noted for their strong beliefs in occult matters and their general pride in their pagan past.

# Icelandic Books of Magic

Other than the collection that came to be called the *Galdrabók,* the once rich tradition of Icelandic magical books of the sixteenth and seventeenth centuries survives only in a fragmentary state. Icelandic folktales report on the existence of famous occult books owned by notorious historical magicians. These kinds of books were also referred to in more reliable historical sources, some of which even contain summaries of their contents. Otherwise we are dependent on later collections, which seem to have carried on the tradition in a living way, and on stray references in manuscripts whose contents generally consist of something other than *galdur.*

According to legend the earliest of the famous Icelandic magicians of the Christian period, Bishop Sæmundur the Wise, is said to have learned the arts of magic at a mysterious "Black School" somewhere in Europe. In later times the two cathedral schools in Iceland, one at Hólar (in the north) and one at Skálholt (in the southwest), were the chief hotbeds of magical activity. As noted before, the legendary material often divides the master magicians into two main types: beneficent and malificent. While Sæmundur the Wise is the model of goodness and Gottskálk the Cruel the archetype of evil, the sources of magical lore are the same (as often from Satan or Óðinn as from the Christian God). In the books and fragments that have survived, all kinds of magic are merrily mixed together. To the magician himself—although not necessarily to the nonmagicians who might sit in judgment of him—magic is a neutral thing that can be used in causes that are either just or unjust, good or evil.

## LEGENDARY BLACK BOOKS

There are two main texts that have assumed mythic importance in the history of Icelandic black books. It is impossible to tell where legend ends and history begins with these accounts, but one thing that is borne out by hard evidence is the *importance* of such books and the overall nature of their contents.

The most famous and sinister of all these books was Rauðskinna (Red-Skin). This was said to have been compiled by the most evil of all magicians, Bishop Gottskálk Niklásson the Cruel, the bishop of Hólar who died in 1520. Rauðskinna is said to be a book of the blackest magic, drawn from the Heathen Age. It was supposed to have been inscribed with golden letters and runes on red parchment. This is why the book was called "Red-Skin," in other words, "Red Vellum." Legend has it that Gottskálk was buried with the Rauðskinna, and it is further said that he did not pass on all of the magic compiled in the book. For this reason the text was thought to possess enormous secret power. Approximately two hundred years after Gottskálk's death, a young scholar named Loftur, or Galdra-Loftur, lived and studied at the school of Hólar. Loftur wished to acquire all the knowledge contained in Rauðskinna. To do this he attempted to raise the dead Gottskálk and force him to give up the book. Even though Loftur was able to raise the dead bishop, he was ultimately unsuccessful in gaining the book. Loftur was left psychologically shattered by the encounter with the powerful ghost of Gottskálk the Cruel. The exact details of this encounter are reported in chapter 7.

Another famous magical book of semi-legend was Gráskinna (Gray-Skin). There were perhaps at one time two different books by this name, one at Hólar and one at Skálholt. The description of this book is interesting in that the text is supposed to have been divided into two parts. The first was written in normal letters (the Roman alphabet) and contained information on lesser magical arts; for example, *glímugaldur* (wrestling magic) and *lófalist* (palmistry). The second part was said to be written in *villurúnir* (deceptive or coded runes designed to conceal their actual meanings). These were black magic spells that the magician Galdra-Loftur is reported to have mastered.

Of course these books may have never actually existed, but certainly ones with contents very much like those described in folktales did exist. We do not need to repeat what the usual fate was for such books once they were discovered by the established authorities. Given the active campaign that was carried out against such books for centuries, it is remarkable any of them survive.

## THE *GALDRABÓK*

The title *Galdrabók* has been given to the oldest and most complete of the books of this kind. The original manuscript of this collection of magical spells was written in Iceland beginning sometime during the latter part of the 1500s. It is therefore a product of the Reformation Age. The manuscript is made up of a collection of spells, more or less randomly pieced together. It is not a unified composition or an attempt to teach magic. It is more a recipe book than a manual. As we have the book now, it has been added to by four scribes working over a period of about a hundred years.

The magician who recorded the first few spells in the book lived in Iceland during the latter half of the sixteenth century. Soon after, the book was passed on to another Icelander who added a few more items. It was probably sometime later that a third Icelandic scribe came into possession of the pages and added the last few spells that were actually written in Iceland. This last Icelandic magician, or *galdramaður,* used a cursive style that can be dated to the seventeenth century. What is noteworthy about his additions is that they contain such a rich storehouse of references to the pagan Germanic lore. These sections were written down around 1650, more than half a millennium after the official Christianization of Iceland. Shortly after this third scribe added his spells, the manuscript was taken to Denmark as part of the effort of humanists to collect literary antiquities. In Denmark it appears to have come into the possession of a Danish magician who wrote the last four entries. This Dane seems to have had some access to other Icelandic books of magic, now lost, from which he collected these spells. We suppose this because the language is Icelandic and no parallel Danish material exists.

Danish philologist J. G. Sparfvenfelt acquired the book in 1682. It was later sent to Sweden, where it became a part of that country's ever-growing collection of "Gothic" monuments and manuscripts. In the end it was acquired by the Royal Swedish Academy of Sciences in Stockholm, where it is now preserved.

The contents of the *Galdrabók* demonstrate essentially two different kinds of magic. One kind works by means of a prayer formula in which higher powers are invoked and by which the magical end is effected indirectly. However, this is only the case with a few of the spells in the *Galdrabók.* More common are spells that work as direct expressions of the magician's will. This will is expressed through signs or through written or spoken formulas. Often these methods are combined so that the overall ritual is very similar to the kind practiced in ancient times and reported by Egill Skallagrímsson.

The religious outlook expressed in Icelandic spells is also of some interest. In the older material spells have a predominantly non-Christian or overtly pagan (or even sometimes diabolical) frame of reference. This is not hard to understand, because the general use of magic was consistently connected to the heathen past and with demonic sources by Christian writers. Nevertheless, at the same time there are spells that have a "purely Christian" frame of reference in that they overtly cite Christian figures or use Christian formulas. We use the term "Christian" with caution, because magic in general, especially when practiced by lay individuals, was looked upon with suspicion by the church. The Judeo-Gnostic tradition is also present. These make use of Judaic or Greco-Gnostic formulas, which entered Scandinavian culture along with Christianity, but they cannot be classified as Christian per se. The *Galdrabók* also contains spells that mix overtly Germanic pagan contents with overtly Christian contents. It is possible that in the Protestant period ritualistic Catholic formulas were seen in a light similar to that of pagan ideas, and both fell into the category of "rejected knowledge" and thus became attractive as material for the creation of magical formulas.

## OTHER COLLECTIONS OF MAGIC

Besides the *Galdrabók,* no complete and archaic book of its kind has survived, but there are several books that contain various amounts of interesting magical lore and spells. One of the main problems for research in this area is that all of the sources have not been collected and edited in an organized way.

One old Icelandic "leechbook" (medicinal manual) from the late 1400s has been edited by Kålund. It contains several pages at the beginning that have more magical content than the other material in the book. These pages contain some of the oldest depictions of the *ægishjálmur* (see chapter 9) and similar signs, as well as prayer formulas in which the old divinities (for example, Óðinn [also as Fjölnir], Þórr, Frigg, and Freyja) are mixed together with Judeo-Christian figures.

Starting in the late eighteenth century we have a continuous record of magical manuals composed in the modern period. Most of these actually date from the 1800s, but their contents go back at least to the 1700s. Various elements they contain can be traced back even further, to the medieval period and beyond.

The *Huld Manuscript* is known to have been compiled by Geir Vigfússon of Akureyri, who died in 1880. The spells contained in this collection are, however, much older. For example, many are comparable with those that appear in the *Galdrabók*. In this manuscript most of the *galdrastafir* or *galdramyndir* are given specific names, and instructions for making them are provided.

There is also a collection known as the *Kreddur Manuscript*. This was discovered in Eyjafjörður. It was written (or perhaps copied) in the late nineteenth century, but linguistic evidence clearly indicates that it largely consists of material originally composed in the seventeenth century.

The National Library of Iceland has a vast collection of magical manuscripts in this tradition. Some are in very poor condition. Thankfully, scholars are now beginning to make new editions of them.

## THE TWO TRADITIONS IN THE NORTH

Generally speaking there were two great traditions of magic in the Scandinavian region: one stemming from the indigenous Germanic culture and one coming from the Continent. The dichotomy between these two is not of extreme importance here since we are concentrating on the Icelandic tradition, which was the most culturally conservative of all the Germanic lands and also the one that synthesized the two strands of magic into a harmonious whole. By contrast, in the magical traditions of England and Germany as early as the tenth century, as well as some magical teachings in Sweden during the sixteenth and seventeenth centuries, we find a transmission of virtually pure magical traditions from the Mediterranean into the northern realms. This transmission occurred through the written word, which was sometimes even translated into the vernacular languages of the North. It should also be realized, however, that the "Mediterranean tradition" was by this time a largely artificial and composite one that included elements from Greco-Egyptian, Judeo-Christian, and even Eastern features from various Near Eastern and Indian cults such as Zoroastrianism, Mithraism, and Manicheanism. This highly synthetic set of practices and rituals made headway against the indigenous Northern tradition, not by brute economic and military force and coercion, as was the case with orthodox religion, but by the gentler and far more irresistible power of prestige.

It is in Germany where this whole process was most clear. There we find an early text in Old High German called the *Second Merseburg Charm,* which is the last record of the god Wodan's name being used in a magical context on the Continent. By contrast, in Iceland the use of his name (Óðinn) continues well into the 1700s and beyond. The name also continues to be known in remote regions of Scandinavia and perhaps even in the countryside of England. We do find that in Germany the old folk traditions of magic also continued, although these were to a great extent superficially Christianized. Older magical customs continued to be practiced at the level of the common folk in the countryside, whereas in the cities and university towns the Mediterranean tradition was actually being further developed, articulated, and even refined by German scholars and magicians. These included the semi-legendary Georg (Johann) Faustus (1480–1539?), Albertus Magnus (1193–1280), Theophrastus Bombastus von Hohenheim (Paracelsus) (1493–1541), and Cornelius Agrippa von Nettesheim (1486–1535). Among them the two traditions were merged. An analysis of the German hermetic magicians shows intense interest in the use of local folk traditions. At the same time, however, these folk traditions were being ever more saturated with non-Germanic figures, entities, and techniques that largely supplanted the pagan ones.

Around the year 1600 a Swedish scholar and magician by the name of Johan Bure (Latinized name: Johannes Bureus; 1568–1652) became the living prototype of a new kind of runic operator. He was simultaneously a scientist and a practitioner of magic. In this he was being very much true to the spirit of the Renaissance. Bure absorbed the magical techniques and ideas that were then being imported into the North from the southern climes, but he also reinvestigated local runic traditions. He welded the two together in his own unique system.

As magical symbols, runes were of little influence in the practice of sorcery on the Continent after the beginning of the Middle Ages. But there are two interesting examples of runes found in non-Scandinavian European magical books. The first is in a fourteenth-century Latin language work found in Italy. It is now housed in the British Museum Library (MS Sloane 3854). The work is actually an edition of the Arabic book of magic originally titled *Ghayat al-Hakim*—known in Latin as the *Picatrix.* The Sloane 3854 version contains several unique features not found in the original, while other parts of the original have been left out. At a certain juncture, instructions are provided about "how to write the names of the planets' spiritual forces in a cryptic alphabet."* The characters of this alphabet are called *runae.* The material demonstrates familiarity with runic practice as known in Scandinavia in the Middle Ages. The second work is a fifteenth-century medical manuscript written in the Alemannic dialect of German. It is now stored in the University Library of Prague (MS XXIII F 129). Here we see the use of a version of the Scandinavian medieval runic alphabet as a device for encoding certain phrases and names of secret ingredients employed in magical recipes, as well as certain words in a conjuration of the devil.

Practical magical books continued to be compiled and collected and, we presume, to be used by Icelandic magicians and lay antiquarians right up into the mid-twentieth century. Typically such material was passed secretly from one magician to another in written form, and sometimes it was even passed from a dead magician to his magical heir. However, it was most common for such books to be discovered by hostile surviving family members and immediately destroyed. A new tradition of collection came into vogue in the twentieth century. Books no longer had to be passed secretly from one magician to another. Instead the manuscripts could be collected in libraries, and there they could be viewed and discovered by a new generation of scholars and practitioners.

*See Burnett and Stoklund, "Scandinavian Runes in a Latin Medieval Treatise," 420.

# The Gods of Magic
## *Æsir, Demons, and Christ*

In the practice of Icelandic magic, the magician tended to appeal to every sort of entity he knew of to effect his will. It did not matter whether it was the Christian God, a demon imported to the North through Christianity (such as Beelzebub), or one of the old native gods or goddesses. No one was excluded. All of them were thought of as possible sources of power, and none of them was especially feared.

In the Icelandic tradition the old gods and goddesses of the Germanic peoples had an uncanny way of surviving in the world of magic and folklore. Only isolated sources mention these old deities in the oldest written materials from Germany, England, or even from other Scandinavian areas. But in Iceland we find a widespread and vigorous life for the old gods. The reasons for this should be obvious from what we have already said about the peculiarities of Icelandic socio-religious history.

In what follows we will examine the whole picture of the "theology" and/or "demonology" presented in Icelandic magical texts. It is our main aim to observe the survival of pagan divinities, but we will also look at their relationship and apparent assimilation to the mythomagical figures from the Judeo-Christian tradition, both the ones thought to be evil as well as the ones thought to be good.

## THE PAGAN GODS AND GODDESSES

In every mythic tradition over which Christianity was laid—including the Germanic—pre-Christian divinities survived in at least two ways. The first was by being driven "underground," where they often lived alongside the other rejected entities (classified as demons). The second way was by being assimilated into accepted or established entities. This latter way can be called the syncretic method. It was by far the more common scenario throughout all traditions. Occasionally and for a time the old gods could be identified with Jesus, his disciples, the apostles, and most commonly with various saints and archangels. Sometimes these saints were preexisting ones, but in other cases there was a virtual canonization of the old divinities under new, Christianized names and circumstances. Here we are only concerned with those instances found in magical contexts, but it is worth realizing that this was a general and widespread phenomenon not limited to the area of magic. This whole process deserves its own separate study.

In the Icelandic sources the most vigorously represented of the old gods is the *Galdrafóðr* (Father of Magic), Óðinn. This should not surprise us. His name not only appears in virtually every litany of names of the old gods, but also his *heiti* (Ice.: bynames, or nicknames) often occur as names of magical signs or in other litanies. By way of example, Jón Árnason records a series of six *galdrastafir,* each of which has a distinctive name* (see figure 4.1 on page 34). Of these six names—Freyr, Fjölnir, Fengur, Þundur, Þekkur, and Þrumur—four (2–5) are well-attested *heiti* belonging to Óðinn. These as well as other nicknames of Óðinn that appear in Icelandic black books show that knowledge of the complex lore of Óðinn's various aspects was kept alive, in addition to the more basic ideas about his functions in Norse myth. When we examine these spells we soon discover that Óðinn is found in all sorts of company, and his name is used for a wide spectrum of magical purposes.

*See Árnason, *Íslenzkar Þjóðsögur,* vol. I, 432.

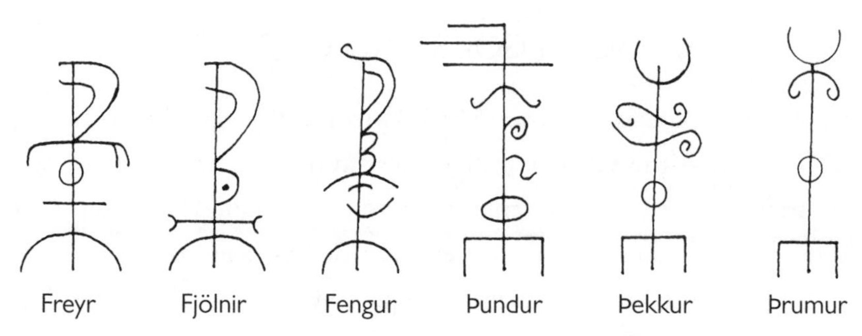


Fig. 4.1. Six *galdrastafir* recorded by Jón Árnason

There is great evidence of continued active knowledge of Óðinn and his magical functions, even if some of this knowledge has been corrupted.

The god Þórr is another one of the old deities who is very actively represented in magical lore. This is not surprising either, as he was the most popular god in pagan Iceland. In the old books of magic his actual name is often represented in litanies of divine and "demonic" names. But there is also evidence that shows that Þórr's magical role in Iceland was most significant through a *galdrastafur* called *Þórshamar* (Þórr's hammer). This name for a sign was actually attached to several different forms over a long span of time. Perhaps originally it was identified with the solar wheel, or swastika. The name and certain variants of the *galdrastafur* are also recorded in the folktale material of Jón Árnason. He shows the form , which is reminiscent of the old solar wheel. Here we are also reminded of the older Viking Age runic inscriptions, which contain the powerful formula *Þórr wigi,* "Þórr sanctify or hallow." Here the idea of sanctifying or hallowing a place (or even the runic inscription and object itself) means that they are protected, set apart from the profane, and empowered by divine force.

In addition to these two highly prominent divinities mentioned in several spells, at least another two of the older divinities' names appear as components of certain herbs. We have *Friggjargras* (Frigg's herb) and another herb is called *Baldursbrá* (Baldur's brow). Frigg was the wife of Óðinn, and Baldur was one of his sons. Baldur was known for his invulnerability and his physical perfection.

One whole myth is obliquely alluded to in spell 46 of the *Galdrabók,* which says: "May you become as weak as the fiend, Loki, who was snared by all the gods." This clearly demonstrates that mythic material otherwise recorded in the *Poetic* and *Prose Eddas* was well known to the *galdramaður* who composed the spell.

Although there are some spells in which single Germanic god names appear, it is more usual for them to be used in litanies of names. There are several things worth noting about these litanies. They contain the names of the great gods and goddesses of the ancient Germanic religion, but they do not seem to be organized in any especially meaningful way with regard to the pagan mythology. Also, the last three of these litanies that appear in the *Galdrabók* (in spells 43, 45, and 46) are really syncretic compositions in which the Germanic names appear right alongside names from Judeo-Christian and Mediterranean myth and magic. However, the overall impression is that the Judeo-Christian elements are newcomers in an already established magical system.

Perhaps one of the most interesting survivals is the name of the dwelling place of the gods, Valhalla (Ice. *Valhöll*). Valhöll is the "hall of the slain" (or perhaps the "hall of the chosen or elect") and is held to be a dwelling place in Ásgarður (court of the gods) in which Odinic warriors who died in battle are honored in the supernal realm. This shows a certain continuance of cosmological traditions from the heathen past, which impressed itself upon the structure of the new entities coming to the North.

## CHRISTIAN DEMONS

Not only are the old gods of the Germanic peoples said to be in Valhöll, but in the view of the *galdramenn* who wrote the *Galdrabók,* so too were the demons of Hebraic mythology—Satan and Beelzebub—to be found there. The most revealing formula is found in spell 43 of the *Galdrabók,* where we read: "Help me in this, all you gods: Þórr, Óðinn, Frigg, Freyja, Satan, Beelzebub, and all those gods and goddesses who dwell in Valhöll." The fact that Satan had come to Valhöll was a significant event in the history of Icelandic magic. This symbolically and eloquently shows how the southern magical elements were at first assimilated in the North on terms set by the Northern tradition.

From the standpoint of the new establishment culture, however, this had the net effect of diabolizing the old Germanic gods. To a great extent, but certainly not exclusively, the old gods were equated with devils in the Christian mind. As time went on, especially beginning at the time the *Galdrabók* was compiled, aggressive magical spells would be more likely to use the old gods or demons in their formulas, whereas protective spells were more likely to make use of Christian elements. This is obviously not a hard-and-fast rule but rather a general tendency.

As noted earlier, the old characteristics and functions of the multifaceted traditional deities were increasingly dichotomized under the influence of the rather Christian dogmas, so for a while the old gods could feel at home alongside either Jesus or Satan. But when all was said and done, because of the nature of Christian doctrine, the old gods and goddesses of Valhöll ultimately found the company of demons more accommodating—at least in a magical context.

It might be convincingly argued that the way had been prepared for this process in Scandinavia centuries earlier. That is because the Christianization of various Indo-European peoples (Greeks, Romans, Celts, and the kindred Germans) was generally accomplished by the same combination of assimilating and diabolizing their native gods. Assimilation, or syncretization, took place covertly, while diabolization and demonization was often quite overt. It is no wonder, then, that the pagan deities of the North—or, more precisely, their sympathizers and followers—would recognize their kith and kin in the guise of the Christian "devils."

On the other hand, and especially in the Catholic period, the new religion was itself heavily impressed with pagan ideas. Certain aspects of the old faith were superficially Christianized, and many of the old traditions were given a Christian veneer. In the world of the magicians this meant that Christian figures could sometimes be used right next to pagan deities. And as our wondrous example in spell 46 of the *Galdrabók* shows, the northern sorcerer was so free magically that he could use the names of Óðinn, the Savior, and Satan in the same litany. This spell, reproduced here for historical purposes only, reads in its entirety:

> Write these staves on white calfskin with your blood. Rouse your blood from your thigh and say: I carve you eight *áss* (runes) [ᚨ], nine *nauð* (runes) [ᚾ], thirteen *þurs* (runes) [ᚦ], which are to afflict your belly with great shitting and shooting pains, and all these may afflict your belly with very great farting. May your posts (= "bones") split asunder, may your guts burst, may your farting never stop, neither day nor night. May you become as weak as the fiend, Loki, who was snared by all the gods. In your mightiest name Lord God, Spirit, Creator, Óðinn, Þórr, Savior, Freyr, Freyja, Oper, Satan, Beelzebub, helper, mighty God, (protect) with your followers Uteos, Morss, Nokte, Vitales.

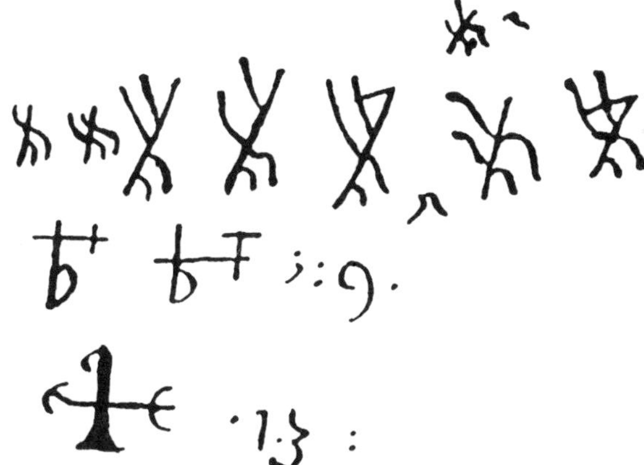

It might also be true that many times when the words "lord" (Ice. *dróttinn*) or "God" (Ice. *guð*) are used, they are not free of heathen connotations, as both words were in full use in pagan times.

It would be a mistake to ignore the many uses of Christian mythology in the historical Icelandic spells. Biblical stories are used as analogical models for magical operations, and the names of various figures from Judeo-Christian myth and legend are used as names of power. It is only important to realize that it is for the sake of power and effectiveness that they are being invoked. A sense of Christian piety is generally absent in the spells as we find them in historical books.

The Icelandic "magical triangle" of Germanic entities, Christian entities, and Christo-demonic entities is a peculiar one in that the old gods remained stronger in Iceland than anywhere else, and they survived most vigorously in magical practice. Even in folktales "old [that is, heathen] knowledge" (Ice. *forneskja* or *fornfræði*) is equated with sorcery. Furthermore, it seems that taken as a whole, and as far as magic is concerned, the demonic entities were never quite as "evil"—nor the Christian figures never quite as "good"—as they seem to have been in other regions.

# Runes and Magical Signs

The knowledge surrounding the ancient lore of the runes had decayed significantly by the sixteenth century. Nevertheless, the history of magic demonstrates that even confused forms can still be used effectively by skilled sorcerers. What most interests us here is the way in which runic magical methods and techniques were handed down in the Icelandic traditions. The two main distinctive graphic features of the Northern style are the use of runes and the magical signs. The runes (Ice. *rúnir*) or runelike symbols, or even magical letters or characters (Ice. *galdra-letur*), were used liberally in Icelandic magical manuals, as were the magical signs known in Icelandic as either *galdrastafir* or *galdramyndir*. As we noted earlier, another striking feature is that the technique by which this magic was effected was often virtually identical with that of the rune magic employed in the pagan age.

Basic runelore is found in appendix A of this book, along with instructions on how to transliterate Old Norse names into authentic runic forms.

As a practical alternative script, the runes continued to be known in Iceland into modern times. They were sometimes used to write inscriptions in and around magical drawings, or to write certain words in spells that the magician wanted to obscure. There was also the use of encoded runic forms called *galdraletur, villuletur,* or *villurúnir.* These were meant to confuse and conceal rather than reveal meanings. Runelore was sometimes used by the magicians who composed or compiled these workings by having certain numbers of runelike figures arranged in a way suggestive of the runic system. For example, efforts were made to use a meaningful number of figures to compose complexes or series of signs, such that there are twenty-four or sixteen or eight of them.

The terminology for describing the magical figures and ways of using them was also inherited from ancient runic magical practice. Often these signs are referred to in Icelandic as *stafir* (sing. *stafur*), "staves." This terminology is taken over from the old technical designation of runes as staves or "sticks." This is because they were from an early time carved on such wooden objects originally used for talismanic or divinatory purposes. The execution of these figures for magical aims is indicated by the Icelandic verbs *rísta* or *rista,* both meaning "to carve, scratch, or cut." At first these terms indicate that actual cutting or carving is intended (into wooden or stone objects, for example), but later they are also used in contexts that show that what is intended is more akin to *writing,* as with ink and quill on parchment or paper.

Certainly the most outstanding single feature of the Icelandic books of magic is the presence of complex magical signs. Most efforts at classifying these signs attempt to determine their relationships to the runes and their magical functions. There are three main types of such signs.

1. *Bandrúnir:* bindrunes made up of more or less obvious combinations of runes
2. *Galdrastafir:* magic staves, which were perhaps originally bind runes but which have become so stylized as to take on independent lives of their own
3. *Galdramyndir:* magical signs that seem to have always been nonrunic, abstract, or iconic signs

Many of the signs appear to be combinations of runes and abstract symbols. The main problem that arises in any effort to decipher these signs is the longstanding tradition of stylization, which can include simplification as well as artificial complication or elaboration. Another way of classifying them has to do with their functions. If they were intended to be protective amulets they might be called by the Latin name *innsigli* (sigils) or by the Icelandic term *varnastafir* (protective staves). The term *galdrastafir* would then indicate magic of an operative nature meant to cause alterations in the environment.

It is almost impossible to read any linguistic meaning in the *galdrastafir* (and many of the *bandrúnir*) without having some indication being given in the commentaries. These leads usually come in the form of the distinctive names given to particular signs. Examples of such names are given in figure 4.1 on page 34. Careful analysis reveals these to be *bandrúnir* that have been stylized in the medium of pen and ink, yet many of their runic features remain visible. On the other hand, many of the names given to magical signs have to do with their functions and not their forms. The names themselves are most often words with highly obscure meanings. The two most famous names of such signs are *ægishjálmur* (helm of awe or terror) and *svefnþorn* (sleep-thorn). The *ægishjálmur* is a name given to a figure that could be simple or extremely complex, but its basic form starts out as a fourfold or eightfold equal-armed cross with branches at its terminals. With these two signs we are lucky, because mythic narratives survive that give us insights into their origins, contexts, and meanings.

The *ægishjálmur* is mentioned in Old Norse literature concerning the legendary hero Sigurðr Fáfnisbani. When Sigurðr slays the serpent named Fáfnir to gain the treasure hoard of the Niflungs (Nibelungen), one of the objects of power that he obtains is the *ægishjálmur*. This is not a "helmet" in the usual sense, but rather a general covering that surrounds the wearer with an overawing power to terrify and subdue any enemies. This power is portrayed as being concentrated between the eyes, and it is often associated with the legendary power of serpents to paralyze their prey. This is an ancient Indo-European concept, as demonstrated by the etymology of the Greek *drakôn*—the "one with the evil eye." This is also reminiscent of the Gorgons' ability to paralyze their victims, to petrify or "turn them to stone," with the gaze of their eyes set in a head surmounted by serpents.

The *svefnþorn* is also mentioned in Old Norse mythic literature as the magical device with which Óðinn placed one of the *valkyrjur,* Sigrdrífa (or Brynhildr), into a deep slumber from which she could be awakened only by one who was able to cross the magical barrier of fire placed around her by Óðinn. This feat too was accomplished by the Odinic hero Sigurðr Fáfnisbani. Spells intended to put people into a deep slumber from which they can be awakened only by the magical will of the sorcerer are common in the Icelandic black books, and there are numerous signs that are given the name *svefnþorn.*

In addition to these two signs there are several other names given to signs, for example, *gapaldur, veðurgapi* ("weather daredevil," to cause a storm), *kaupaloki* ("deal-closer," for good business), *ginnir* (also a name of Óðinn), and *angurgapi* ("reckless one of anger"). The fact that the same name may be attached to two or more different signs shows the names are not so much given to the particular shape of the sign but instead describe the sign's intended effect.

Despite the fact that it is obviously of Mediterranean origin, the so-called *sator*-square has certainly found a lively existence in the magical

**S A T O R**
**A R E P O**
**T E N E T**
**O P E R A**
**R O T A S**

Fig. 5.1. *Sator*-square

lore of the North. As a graphic sign it most often appears inscribed in Latin letters (see figure 5.1 on page 42). The verbal formula was apparently well known, as magical instructions sometimes call for reciting the "*sator-arepo.*" It seems clear that this means that the practitioner is to speak the apparently nonsense sounds *sator-arepo-tenet-opera-rotas*. The *sator*-square formula was so well integrated into Northern practice that it is also found in at least nine runic inscriptions! One example is found on the bottom of a fourteenth-century silver bowl from Dune, Gotland (see figure 5.2, below).

The *sator*-formula is actually one that conceals the formula Paternoster ("Our Father") plus the formula "A + O" (*alpha* + *omega*). This formula is obviously best known as the beginning of the Christian "Lord's Prayer." This prayer is widely used in magical contexts, but the formula actually predates Christianity. We know this because an example of the *sator*-square was found in the ruins of the Roman city of Pompeii—buried under volcanic ash in the year 79 CE. This predates any known Christian influence in that city, and so it demonstrates that the "Our Father" prayer was used by some sect before the advent of organized Christianity. The sect in question was most likely the cult of Mithras from which organized Christianity adopted many features.

Fig. 5.2. Reproduction of the *sator*-square from the Dune bowl

# The Theory and Practice of Galdor-Sign Magic

Examples such as the *sator*-square point up the fact that there were definitely influences coming into the North from the southern European traditions of magic. But to some extent these examples serve also to show the remarkable degree to which basic Northern ideas of how magic works, and of how to work magic, remained intact even under this superficial influence.

We will now look at the underlying theories of magic as expressed in the Icelandic *galdrabækur,* at the powers by which it was thought to work, and at some of the consistent ritual techniques.

Standard medieval magical theories stemming from the Mediterranean and Middle East are based on a model in which lower entities are coerced by the agency of higher entities to fulfill the wishes of the magician. This usually involves long preparations, and the magician must also use specific ritual procedures to ensure protection from the entities that he invokes. After the rite the magician formally banishes the spirits he has invoked. There are certain aspects of this theoretical working model that remain foreign to the Icelandic magician. In Icelandic magic it is rare to see any extensive preparations indicated for a specific working; instead it appears that the magician constantly prepared himself in a general way and then applied his spells almost in a rough-and-ready fashion. This is very reminiscent of the way Egill Skallagrímsson worked. Furthermore, the Icelandic magician never seems to need to protect himself from the powers upon which he is calling; to the contrary, he appears more concerned with the actions of other humans. Although spiritual entities are involved, it would be more accurate to say that they *help* the magician work his own will rather than do the work for him—and because the magician has no need to protect himself from the entities he summons, he has no need to banish them.

Generally speaking, Icelandic magic seems to have worked through one of three media: (1) graphic signs, (2) spoken or written words, and (3) natural substances. These media could be used alone or in combination with one another.

Graphic signs (including runes and other written or drawn characters) are thought to be conduits or doorways through which various impersonal powers or personalized entities are directed in order to facilitate the will of the magician. The actual physical sign seems to have little power on its own; it is only in combination with the will of a trained magician that any results can be expected. That is why, in the folktales concerning the famous *galdramenn,* such emphasis is placed on their scholarly characters and on the fact that signs had to be learned by a process that apparently involved more time and effort than just memorizing their external forms. Nevertheless, the memorization of their forms was likely the first step in this process. Except for the most common signs such as the *ægishjálmur* or the *Þórshamar,* specific "staves" rarely appear more than once among the various manuscripts. The fact that quite different staves might be called by the same name, however, indicates that it was an inner form—rather than an external shape—that was mainly being "learned."

Words, whether spoken or written, are the medium often used to activate the signs. Words can work alone either to direct or command some power or entity or to beseech an entity to act on behalf of the magician. The latter prayer-type formula is usually found only in spells of a Christianized kind. In the medieval Icelandic formularies words and names can activate the corresponding power or entity in a way desired by the magician and as formulated in his verbal spell. The "power of the name" is a well-known phenomenon in the annals of magic, and such a belief was also part of the ancient Germanic worldview. Its most famous depiction is in the lore surrounding Sigurðr Fáfnisbani: after fatally wounding the serpent Fáfnir, Sigurðr attempts to conceal his name from the dying giant because, as we read in the "Fáfnismál," a poem from the *Poetic Edda,* "it was the belief in olden times that the words of a doomed man had great might, if he cursed his foe by name."* This ancient Germanic lore was, of course, further reinforced by the importation of Judeo-Gnostic names of God or words of power that are heaped up in some of the Christian-type spells. In all cases these verbal elements are seen as being vitally linked to the actual things they name, and therefore willful and trained manipulation of such words and names constitutes a manipulation of the actual things or entities.

Certain substances tend to be used in magical operations, the most typical being blood and woods of various kinds. Both are well represented in the heathen type of spell. The blood of the magician can be used, and in the old material four kinds of wood—oak, rowan, alder, and ash—are frequently mentioned. Herbs are also referenced in many old spells. The most useful are *millefolium* (yarrow) and *Friggjargras* (*Platanthera hyperborea*). Many other spells make use of various substances on which staves are to be carved or written. In each case there seems to be an underlying analogical reason for the use of the substance, which must be evaluated on a case-by-case basis.

In Icelandic magical spells emphasis is laid heavily on the person of the magician. He is rarely said to have the explicit help of outside forces, and the rituals, such as they are, are quite simple procedures.

*See "Fáfnismál," prose following st. 1, in Hollander, trans., *The Poetic Edda,* 223. Folke Ström devoted a whole study, titled *Den döendes makt och Oden i trädet,* to the magical power of the speech of the dying man.

This is, again, a sharp contrast to the multilateral complexities found in grimoires of the southern tradition.

Because there is such a strong emphasis placed on the person of the magician, it is necessary to take a closer look at what makes up the psychophysical complex of the individual human being. We can know this to a fairly exact degree because they had such a well-developed set of technical terms for the psyche. In pagan times this body-soul structure could have been described as having

1. a physical body (ON *lík*)
2. a shape or semiphysical body image (ON *hamr*)
3. a faculty of inspiration (ON *óðr*)
4. a vital breath (ON *önd*)
5. a volitive/cognitive/perceptive faculty (ON *hugr*)
6. a reflective faculty (ON *minni*)
7. a "shade," or after-death, image (ON *sál* or, figuratively, *skuggi,* "shadow")
8. a permanent magical soul or fetch (ON *fylgja*)
9. a dynamistic empowering substance that gives luck, protection, and the ability to shape-shift (ON *hamingja*)

Unfortunately, with the coming of Christianity, this refined native psychology, or "soul lore," was assailed and began to decay and became very confused and stunted. In our *galdrabækur* we have only the remnants of a fragmented system. Nevertheless, it is clear that the Icelandic magicians preserved some of the technical lore in ways they believed magic worked. It seems fairly clear that even in the period in which those spells were being used the magicians recognized (1) an animating or vital principle, (2) a personal image, (3) a separable power entity by which "sendings" (Ice. *sendingar*) were projected, and (4) an essential core faculty of "heart and mind" (Ice. *hugur*).

For example, it is obvious that curse formulas are meant to deplete the vital energy of a person or animal, and protective formulas are meant to build up this faculty. Other formulas are intended to change the quality of the contents of the *hugur*—for example, to cause someone to fear or love the magician. The ability to see shades, or images, of other people, especially ones who have stolen something from the magician, is also frequently mentioned.

For the form of magic outlined in the practical parts of this book some command over these faculties must first be developed. Without this development the words and signs are mere empty shells that await vivification by the faculties of a developed magician.

Spell 34 in the *Galdrabók,* adapted in this book as a spell to acquire love, represents a working to get the love of a woman. It is an attempt to turn her free will genuinely toward the magician, but it is couched in the magical forms of threats and curses. A review of the magical procedures would include a complex set of actions. First, the woman's being is linked to the formula by means of location (placing the staves and material components of the spell "in a place where she will go over it") and essence (writing her name with staves); then the magician's (sexual) being is linked with the woman's being and with the magical formulas by means of the "etin-spear blood" ("snake blood," that is, semen); and finally, the magical signs that graphically embody the aim of the operation are inscribed and the whole contained in a ring of water. All of this has linked the woman, the magician, and the aim in an essential but as yet only general way. This symbolic and graphic series of actions and signs is then empowered and given a specific direction by means of the words spoken over the forms. This spell includes references to how the formula is to work within the psychological scheme as understood by the magician. It includes graphic imagery and a prayerlike entreaty to Óðinn for success. (In the ancient mythology, Óðinn is, by the way, known for his interest in spells of this kind.) Just about all of the elements common to medieval Icelandic spells are to be found in this operation, and again, it should not be missed that the general procedure is quite the same as that practiced by the pagan runic magicians of the North.

Ultimately it must be said that the theory of galdor-sign magic is one in which there is a system of communication between the magician and the causal powers of the universe. All systems of communication have their own language, and hence grammar, by which precise messages can be sent and received by the various parties involved. If this language is learned, the code of grammar and vocabulary is "cracked"; the magician is then free to conduct his or her own communications as desired. Here we learn to communicate with causal powers through the signs: we send messages in signs and the universe responds with events, either inner or outer ones in ourselves or in the minds of others. We basically do this in a manner similar to the way we learn and speak our own native languages of natural communication. The first step is to observe how the process works. This is then followed by a period of imitating the successful communications of others, after which we can begin to finally communicate on our own, in ways that are effective for us. This book guides you through the first two levels of this process and shows you a glimpse of the third. But the third level is one that must be undertaken independently.

Languages are made up of increasingly complex levels of signs. At the base level we start with phonology, the understanding of the system of basic *sounds* in the language. The next level is morphology, the understanding of the meaningful clusters into which sounds can be arranged, basically what we call "words." Syntax is the next level, which has to do with the arrangement of words in meaningful strings to convey a more complex communication: the sentence. Galdor signs work in a similar way, just in more dimensions than natural language. In chapter 9 of this book we will go into the practical aspects of this grammar of the galdor signs.

# The Legends and Lore of Iceland's Magicians

The student of Icelandic magic is lucky to have so many resources available to learn about the art of galdor. We have the books of magic, as well as a good idea about the people who practiced this form of magic. We can also study its deeper background. One of the most valuable resources is the rather substantial folklore surrounding the magicians who were active at the time this form of magic was taking shape. What follows here is a series of translations of actual Icelandic folklore material. They are arranged in roughly chronological order with regard to the time periods in which the magician lived. All of the individuals described are actual historical persons, but the events surrounding their lives may have been embellished by myth and legend. This represents a short selection of material that exists in Icelandic literature.

## SÆMUNDUR THE WISE (1056–1133)

Sæmundur the Wise sailed overseas and attended the Black School (*Svartiskóli*), and there he learned strange arts. There was no schoolmaster to be seen in the Black School, but whatever the students might want to know about in the evening, books about this would be provided the next morning, or otherwise it might be written up on the walls.

Above the entrance, on the inner side, was written: "You may come in; your soul is lost." There was a law in that school that anyone who came must study there for three years. All the ones who were leaving in any given year had to leave the place at the same time, and the devil would always keep the one who was last to leave, and so they would always draw lots to see who would be last one out. More than once the lot fell on Sæmundur, and so he stayed there longer than the law allowed.

But then it so happened that Bishop Jón was traveling to Rome and passed nearby. He found out that Sæmundur was still at the Black School for the aforementioned reason, so he went in and spoke to Sæmundur and offered to help him escape, provided he would go to Iceland and behave as a good Christian. Sæmundur accepted these terms. Bishop Jón made Sæmundur walk in front of him, but he wore his cloak loosely over his shoulders, and just when Jón was about to get out, a hand came up through the floor and gripped the cloak and pulled it under, but Jón got out.

After this the devil (*fjandinn*) came to Sæmundur and made a pact (*kontrakt*) with him: if Sæmundur could remain hidden for three nights he would be free, but if not, he would belong to him. The first night Sæmundur hid under a riverbank, both in the water and in the soil at the same time, thus the devil (Satan) thought that Sæmundur had drowned in the river; the second night he hid out at sea in a shipwreck that was drifting offshore, so the devil believed that the river must have spit him out into sea; the third night he had himself buried in consecrated earth, so the devil thought that Sæmundur must have been washed ashore dead and been buried in a churchyard, into which he dared not go to seek him. All this was done according to Bishop Jón's advice.

Other people say that this is how Sæmundur escaped: His fellow students made a deal with him that he would go out last; so he sewed a leg of mutton to the hem of his cloak, and as he followed the group who were rushing out through the school doors something grabbed at the cloak and caught the leg. Then Sæmundur dropped the cloak and took off on foot, saying, "He grabbed, but I slipped away," and so he rejoined his fellow students.

## GOTTSKÁLK THE CRUEL (1497–1520)

Bishop Gottskálk the Cruel was the greatest magician of his time; he renewed the practice of black magic (*svartagaldur*), which had not been in customary use since pagan times, and compiled a book of magic that was called Red-Skin (Rauðskinna). It was written with gold letters and was highly embellished; it was inscribed with rune staves just like all magic spells. The bishop would grant this book to no one after his day, and for this reason he had the book buried with him and did not teach all of his magical knowledge to anyone. Therefore he was harmful to everyone by way of his speech so that he could confuse the memories and minds of men to get them to do things for which he could blame them. At first he thought to hire spies to find out who was eating meat during the Lenten fast, but in the end no one wanted to conduct espionage for him. One man alone was sufficient to do the job, so the bishop taught him magic tricks (*kukl*), and among these was the donning of the helm of hiding (*hulins hjálmur*); although he did not teach him more so that he could control him.

One time during the Lenten fast this spy went to the farm of a certain farmer and positioned himself at the window of the sitting room; it was very dark outside so the spy did not take heed and did not think it necessary to put on the helm of hiding. But the farmer saw more in front of his face than a certain somebody knew; the farmer saw how the spy came and positioned himself at the window. He then asked his wife where the side of mutton was that they had left uneaten at Shrovetide eve. His wife became angry and asked whether he knew what was at stake, but he said that they had nothing to worry about and ordered her to go fetch the meat. At that point the woman dared not do anything but what she was ordered to do and fetched the meat, and she said, "This is a good fat morsel." She took the meat and then took a long, pointed knife and cut through the meat. The light burned dully and the spy-man crouched down at the window to see everything that was to be seen. The farmer went about everything indifferently; he lifted the side of mutton up high and looked at it on every side, but the other man did not see the knife. But when least expected the farmer turned to the window and thrust the knife, which was sticking out of the side of mutton, through the windowpane into the eye of his guest so that it stuck in deep and said, "Take this bite I'm giving you!" The spy let out a scream and fell down. The farmer got the true story out of him, and then the spy died in great agony.

The farmer brought this case before the magistrate Jón Sigmundsson. They went to the bishop, who was unprepared before he had learned the fate of his messenger, and although he denied any responsibility he saw that it was most advisable to pay the farmer a lot of money, and the magistrate Jón passed the judgment that anyone who would lurk outside a window had no rights. From that time on the bishop was not able to force different men to get money from farmers but only to intimidate them into paying out when he saw by his magic that they had not paid everything they owed. Although the bishop never got annoyed with the farmer who killed his spy, because he knew he could not win, he did persecute Jón the magistrate, because he could not help himself, and he did not stop until he had made the magistrate penniless. So Jón vexed himself to death, but at the hour of his own death he summoned the bishop to God's judgment, and the bishop could not see this by means of his magic because one stronger than him intervened.

## EIRÍKUR OF VOGSÓSAR (1638–1716)

There are four versions presented below of the Eiríkur of Vogsósar stories.

### *1. How Eiríkur Learned His Arts at School*

At Biskupstungar there was once an old cottager who was heathen (*forn*) in his ways; he seldom mixed with other people. He owned two things that he thought were better than all of his other possessions. These were a book, of which no one else knew the contents, and a young cow that he fed very well. The old man got very ill and sent word to the bishop of Skálholt and asked him to come and see him. The bishop quickly set out, thinking it would be best to talk to the man about a few things, and so he went to meet him. The cottager said, "The way things are going, my lord, I will soon be dead, and I want to make a little request of you first." The bishop agreed.

The cottager said, "I own a book here, and a young cow that I love very much, and I want to have them both in my grave with me. If not, things will be the worse for everybody."

The bishop tells him that this will be done, for he thought it could be expected that the old man would walk again after death if it were not done. Then the old man died, and the bishop had him buried with his book and his young cow.

Many years later there were three students at the Cathedral School at Skálholt who undertook to learn magic (*fjölkynngi*). One of them was named Bogi, the second Magnús, and the third Eiríkur. They had heard talk about the old man and his book, and they very much wanted to possess that book. So one night they went out to awaken the old cottager from the dead, but no one could tell them where his grave was. So they decided to go through the graves row by row, raising the dead from each, one after the other; they filled the whole church with ghosts (*draugar*), but the old man did not come. Therefore they put them all to rest again and filled the church a second time, and then a third, and then there were only a few graves left, and the cottager had not appeared. When they had put all the other ghosts to rest they raised these last ones, and the very last to appear was the cottager, and he had his book under his arm and was leading his young cow. They all rushed toward the old man; they wanted to get the book, but he fought hard, and all they could do was to defend themselves, although they did snatch a few pages from the first part of the book but gave up on obtaining any more of the rest. Then they wanted to put to rest all those who were still lurching about, and they succeeded with everyone except the old man. They got nowhere at all with him; he was still trying to get back the lost part of his book. But they held their own, though they had their work cut out to do so, and this went on until daybreak. But when the day dawned, the cottager disappeared into his grave, and they chanted (*þuldu*) their spells (*fræði*) over it, and the old man was not seen again. But the three students kept the leaves from his book for their own use, and based on them they put together the book of magic (*fjölkynngisbók*) named Gray-Skin (*Gráskinna*) and it remained for many years on a table in the Cathedral School at Skálholt; Bogi gained the most from this, for he learned more than the others.

Later these three students were ordained into the priesthood, and Eiríkur became the priest of Vogsósar in Selvogur . . .

Although the fellows had kept their learning of magic (*fjölkynngislærdóm*) concealed (*dult*), it was not long before word got around that Eiríkur was a magician (*göldróttur*), so his bishop summoned him and showed him Gray-Skin and ordered him to make a clear statement as to whether he was acquainted with what was in it. Eiríkur flicked the pages and said, "I don't know a single one of these signs (*staf*) in here," and this he solemnly swore and then went back home. But afterward he told his friends that he knew all the signs, except just one single one.

### *2. How Eiríkur Learned His Arts at School (a variation)*

When Eiríkur was at school at Skálholt, some of the students decided to awaken the ghost of an old man buried in the churchyard there, who had owned a magic book of great power. They raised and eventually confined him, but none of them could get the book out from under his arm until Eiríkur approached him, whereupon the book loosened from his grip at once. Eiríkur read in it until shortly after dawn. Then he shut it and gave it back to its owner, who took it and quickly sank back into his grave. Later the other students asked him what he had read. "Enough," he said, "to know that if I had read any more I would have lost my soul to the devil."

### *3. Eiríkur's Pupil and the Book*

Many young schoolboys would go to Eiríkur and ask him to teach them. He tested (*reyndi*) them in various ways and would teach the ones who satisfied him. Among others, there was a boy who requested instruction in magic (*í galdri*). Eiríkur said, "Be here with me until Sunday and then accompany me to Krýsuvíkur; afterward I will tell you whether you are in or out."

On Sunday they rode off. But when they got out to the sands, Eiríkur says, "I have forgotten my handbook; it is under my pillow. Go and fetch it, but do not open it."

The boy went and fetched the book and rode back out to the sands. Now he felt a longing to look inside the book, and this he does. A countless host of devils (*púkar*) came toward him, asking, "What has to be done? What has to be done?" He answered quickly, "Make a rope from the sand!" They got to work, but he continued on his way and catches up to the priest out on the lava fields. The priest took the book and said, "You opened it." This the boy denied. They went on their intended way, but on the return trip the priest saw where the devils (*púkar*) were sitting on the sands.

Then he said, "I knew you had opened the book, my good fellow, although you denied it; but you came up with the best possible plan, and it would be worthwhile teaching you."

And thus it is said that he did teach him.

### *4. Raising Ghosts (a variation)*

Once two boys came to Eiríkur the priest and asked him to show them how he went about awakening ghosts (*draugar*). He asked them to come with him to the churchyard. This they did. He murmured something under his breath, and there came a gush of earth up out of a grave. But each of the boys reacted differently: one laughed but the other cried.

Eiríkur said to the latter, "Go back home, my good fellow, and give thanks that you still have your wits about you; the second boy would be a pleasure to teach."

But it is not known whether anything came of this.

## GALDRA-LOFTUR (DIED 1722)

There was a student at Hólar named Loftur who was always studying magic and who made some of his fellow students take up the study as well, although the others never got any further than some basic tricks (*kukl*). Loftur asked his fellow students to perform magical jokes on other people, and he was himself the leading practitioner of this. One time Loftur went home at Yuletide to his parents' house; for this purpose he took a serving girl from the place, put horseshoes and a bridle on her, and thus rode her in a magical ride (*gandreið*) there and back. She had to remain in bed for a long time afterward suffering from wounds and exhaustion, and she was unable to talk about this as long as Loftur was alive. Another time there Loftur got a servant woman pregnant and then killed the mother of his child with workings (*gjarningar*). She was used to carrying bowls to and from the kitchen, and for the sake of speed some women would carry a sort of tray-shaped instrument known as a "bowl float" in which they would carry many bowls at once. Loftur had a passageway open up in front of her in the middle of a wall, and she went into it. Because of this the girl became frightened and hesitated so the magic worked and the wall closed up again. A long time afterward, when the wall was torn down, the skeleton of a woman was found standing upright with a bunch of bowls in her arms and the skeleton of an unborn child in the cavity of her body.

Reverend Þorleifur Skaftason, because he was the rural dean and the cathedral vicar, rebuked Loftur for his behavior. Nevertheless, Loftur did not change his ways. In fact, Loftur now began to try to harm the dean, although he could not harm him because Reverend Þorleifur was such a great man of God that nothing impure (*óhreint*) could do him harm. One time the dean was on his way to church and had to cross the Hjaltadal River when it was rushing during of the spring thaws. In midstream his horse became frightened and stalled, so the dean grabbed his bag with his cassock in it, dismounted, and waded ashore. He was not harmed and held mass services later that day. The following verse was composed about this.

*On his own two feet he came*
*(the news came as a shock),*
*Then home to Hólar he came,*
*Carrying his cassock.*

Loftur did not let up until he had learned everything that was in Gray-Skin, and he knew it in detail; he then sought advice from various other magicians, but no one knew more than he did. He then grew so jaded and evil in temper that all the other boys in the school were afraid of him and dared not do anything except allow it to be as he wished, no matter how much they might be opposed to it.

One time in the early winter Loftur started speaking to a boy whom he knew to be courageous and asked him to help him awaken the ancient bishops from the dead. This boy hesitated, but Loftur said he would kill him. So the boy asked how he could possibly help him, as he did not know any magic (*galdur*).

Loftur told him that he only needed to stand in the bell tower and hold on to the bell rope, not moving at all, and stare steadily at him and ring the bell at once when he gave him a sign with his hand.

Loftur now said, "I want to tell you about my plans. Those who have learned as much magic as I have can only use it for evil, and must all be destroyed when they die. But if a man knows enough, then the devil (*djöfullinn*) will have no power over the man, but rather he must be his servant without receiving anything in return, just as he served Sæmundur the Wise, and whoever knows as much as that is also his own master (*sjálfráður*), able to use his knowledge (*kunnáttu*) however he wishes. This knowledge is not easy to obtain in this day and time, since the Black School (*Svartiskóli*) closed down, and Gottskálk the Cruel had his book, Red Skin, buried with him. That is why I want to wake him up and force him by magic (*særa*) to hand Red Skin over to me, but all the old bishops will also rise with him, for they will not be able to resist the powerful conjurations (*særingar*) as well as Gottskálk will. So I will make them tell me all the old lore (*forneskja*) they knew in their lifetimes, which is not a problem for me, as I can tell right away by looking whether a man knew magic (*galdur*) or not. I cannot awaken the later bishops, because they were all buried with the Scripture on their breasts. Serve me well and do as I ask you; do not ring too soon or too late, for my life and my eternal welfare depend on it. I will reward you so well that no man will be your superior."

They gave their word on this and got up soon after bedtime and snuck out into the cathedral. The moon was shining so brightly outside that the church was bright inside; the schoolboy stopped in the bell tower, while Loftur went on into the pulpit and began to conjure (*særa*). Soon a man rose up through the floor, serious but with a mild expression, and he wore a crown. The boy thought for sure that this must have been the first bishop of Hólar.

He said to Loftur, "Stop this, you wretched man, while there is time, for my brother Gvendur's prayers will weigh down heavily upon you if you bother him."

Loftur ignored him and continued to conjure. Then, one by one, all the ancient bishops rose up from their graves, all in priestly vestments, with pectoral crosses, and carrying croziers. All said a little something to Loftur, but it is not known what was said. Three of them wore crowns; the first, the last, and the middle one. None of them was concealing any magic lore (*forneskja*).

Gottskálk resisted this, and Loftur now began to conjure him in real earnest, turning his speech to Gottskálk alone; then he turned to the penitential psalms of David rededicated to the devil and made a confession of all the good he had ever done as if it were sin instead. The three crowned bishops now stood at the other end of the church with their hands uplifted and turned their faces toward Loftur, while the others looked away from all of them. Then a great rumbling was heard, and a man rose up through the floor with his crozier in his left hand and a red book under his right arm; he did not have a pectoral cross. He cast an unfriendly eye toward the other bishops and then turned and grinned at Loftur, who was now conjuring as hard as possible. Gottskálk moved a bit closer and said in a sarcastic tone, "Well sung, son, and better than I thought you would, but you won't get my Red-Skin."

Hearing this, Loftur turned himself inside out with rage and conjured as he had never done before. He gave the benediction and recited the Lord's Prayer, both with the name of the devil (*djöfulinn*), until the whole church shook and rocked as if in an earthquake. To the other boy it seemed that Gottskálk edged nearer to Loftur and unwittingly reached a corner of the book out to him. Before this he had been frightened, but now he shook with terror and everything turned black before his eyes, but it seemed to him that the bishop held up the book and that then Loftur stretched out his hand to grab it. At this moment he thought Loftur had given him the signal and he pulled the bell rope, and at once all the dead sank back down through the floor, with a great rushing noise.

Loftur stood in the pulpit for a brief moment as if he were paralyzed and put his head in his hands, and then he stumbled down and found his comrade, went up to him, and said, "Now this went worse than it should have, but I don't blame you. I could well have waited for the dawn, when the bishop would have had to give the book up, and he would have handed it over to me, since he would have to have made this payment to be allowed to get back into his grave, nor would this have been allowed by the other bishops. But he was more enduring than I in the contest between us, because when I saw the book and heard his mockery I became enraged (*óður*) and thought I could get it immediately by force of conjurations (*særingar*); I came to my senses when, if I had chanted just one conjure-stave (*særingarstafur*) more, it would have sunk the whole cathedral into the ground, which is what he intended. In that moment I saw the faces of the crowned bishops, and so faltered, but I knew that you would turn weak and grasp the bell rope to sound the bell, while the book was so close to me that I felt I could grasp it. As it was I touched the corner, and I really did think I had got a grip on it and would never drop it! But things have to go as they have been ordained (*auðið*), and now my salvation is lost forever—and your reward as well. We must both keep quiet about it."

After this experience Loftur is said to have become ever more depressed and fearful. He left school and sought solace from a nearby priest who specialized in helping people recover from magical attacks. At first the priest stayed with Loftur day and night, but after a while the boy seemed to be doing better. The priest left one day and made Loftur promise not to go outdoors while he was away. Loftur promised, but soon after the priest left the boy went to a nearby fisherman and had him row his boat out into the calm sea. Witnesses report that a large gray hand thrust up from the sea and dragged the boat to the depths. No sign was ever found of Loftur, the fisherman, or his boat.

# Preparation and Inner Work

To practice the art of galdor signing properly and effectively, there are some preparations that have to be made. The lesser preparations are outer ones: a certain space must be dedicated to galdor work and certain objects suitable for the practice of the art must also be obtained. The ritual space need only be a clear and neat space on a desk or table. This does not need to be a special ritual table or altar. Galdor-stave magic is too pragmatic to require such things. There are also a number of tools that should be on hand to execute the staves and signs, such as pens (the kind used for calligraphy is ideal), parchment or paper, a straightedge (ruler), a compass (optional), and some candles—red, white, and black. These tools will be discussed in the next chapter.

What is more important are the mental or inner preparations that must take place before success in galdor-sign magic can be expected on any routine basis. One should undertake a curriculum of regular exercises in concentration and visualization such as the one outlined in my book *The Nine Doors of Midgard* (see bibliography under Thorsson, Edred). A special skill, and one that has to be learned, is that of memorizing the visual shapes and details of the *galdrastafir.* The various texts and verbal formulae that are often repeated in the practice of this magic should likewise be memorized. These skills of concentration, visualization, and memorization are ones that ancients took for granted and that modern people almost entirely neglect—they have machines to do all that for them. This negligence is often at the root of magical failure.

When the galdor men of old would say that they wanted "to learn a sign" (Ice. *að læra einn staf*) it meant something very specific. To *learn* a sign meant that it was (1) impressed into their visualized memories such that they could reproduce it without reference to an outwardly visible model or copy, (2) they had learned how to *activate* the sign by visualizing it in *action,* and (3) they had learned (and memorized) the verbal formulae that accompanied the sign.

The first point speaks to the level of memory and concentration necessary to begin to practice this kind of magic. The second point refers to the talent the mind must develop for seeing two-dimensional objects in three and ultimately four dimensions. This faculty must be learned and practiced. All *galdrastafir* are two-dimensional representations of higher-dimensional keys to the transformation and modification of events. Finally, the verbal or other formulas of action must, of course, be learned. This last element is often seen as the most important part of the process, but the secret is that it is *not*—rather, it is the second element that really makes the sign work. The verbal component and other ritual actions seal and give final direction to the effects of the vivified sign. All of the three phases are, however, indispensable to one another.

This threefold ritual of drawing a sign from memory, visualizing its activated higher-dimensional model, and directing or sealing its effects verbally or through other ritual action is a powerful act of mental synthesis. Memory, concentration, and visualization are all focused in this act. Eventually, such magic can be practiced without even using visible models.

Success in magic or sorcery goes beyond just getting results and proving to yourself that "magic really works." Often success in just getting something to happen ends in ultimate disaster, because the wrong things were "wished for." The resulting short-term "success" becomes a long-term failure.

Ask yourself: Am I *wise* enough to practice operant sorcery? How do I *know* that I am actually aware of what it is that I *need*? What if I am stuck with the result of a powerful working of sorcery for the rest of my life? The answer to these questions lies in the concept of *initiation*. Most of magical effort should be spent in gaining knowledge, wisdom, and self-transformation. Most of your woes will be healed when this process is successful. However, certain emergencies in life require that the magician be proficient in sorcery. Experiment with caution and careful consideration.

Here a final warning is given because this form of sorcery is so effective. Any practitioner is urged to use it with careful consideration and wisdom. We are all reminded of Mickey Mouse in *Fantasia*—a representation of the age-old myth of the sorcerer's apprentice. If the power to change events exceeds the practitioner's wisdom to apply that power, disaster will inevitably strike. The same lesson is taught in the stories of Rabbi Loew and the golem or in that of Frankenstein and his monster. Most would-be sorcerers are protected by their own incompetence or lack of talent, the complexity and impracticability of the magical system with which they are working, or the incompleteness of the instructions they have been given. In the Gray-Skin section of this book you have a simple, complete set of instructions. For this reason I urge you to use it with wisdom, for your own protection.

For all of the reasons given above, workings to gain wisdom and knowledge appear early in the Gray-Skin section of this book. These are really the most important signs in the entire corpus, for with their successful performance and learning, no other workings will really be necessary.

# Ritual and the Grammar of Signs

## INTRODUCTION

By its very nature Icelandic galdor-sign magic is very pragmatic and outwardly simple. Inwardly, it is more complex and difficult. It does not require the memorization of long texts, the acquisition of many rare ingredients, or expensive magical tools or weapons. But at its highest level there is a requirement for precise and powerful inner skill and execution. This requirement applies to all forms of magic, but in the case of so-called high magic it is often obscured by the outer complexities of the ceremonial format. For the sign magic to work best, it is also optimal if the signs are drawn from *memory* rather than copying them from other books.

In the case of galdor-stave magic, the ritual is an inner set of events, supported by a minimum of outer actions. Ultimately, a successful galdor-sign magician will be able to visualize and quicken signs in his or her imagination and cause events to occur or alter the psychological perspectives of others.

## EQUIPMENT

***Pens:*** In the early modern period, the scribes of the old books of magic would have used quills dipped in ink or fountain pens. The modern practitioner can use any kind of pen that he or she finds aesthetically pleasing and effective. A pen with a broad nib (such as the kind used for calligraphy) will be able to reproduce the look of the old signs better than others, but this is not necessary. Some may use pens of different colors, black, red, or green being the most common.

***Parchment or paper:*** Most signs are drawn on parchment or paper. You can acquire genuine parchment (made from sheepskin) or vellum (made from calfskin) for a more authentic traditional experience, but parchmentlike paper can also serve well. Normal paper is also fine. The importance usually does not lie in the substance of the medium. The old instructions sometimes tell you to use certain items, but as often as not these were things that would have been readily available at the time and place the original books were written.

***Straightedge:*** Many signs are made up of straight lines. To do these well, a straightedge object should be used. This can be a piece of wood or a ruler.

***Compass:*** This tool is only necessary some of the time. When exact circles are needed or desired, it is the instrument to use.

***Candles:*** Three candles—white, red, and black—are used on the ritual table to illuminate the working space. Working with such a source of illumination is more conducive to gaining the right mental state than is electric light.

Various individual workings will be found to have specific requirements for tools or substances such as water, certain kinds of wood, and so on. When it is necessary to carve a sign on wood, a knife can be used or a sharp stylus is also traditional. Other ritual items necessary to the basic working are clear and should be prepared ahead of time for the working. In general, because of the pragmatic theory of Icelandic galdor-stave magic, ordinary household objects can be brought to bear for magical use. The magic comes from inside the soul of the practitioner.

## BASIC RITUAL FORMAT

As has been mentioned above, the simplest outer form of a galdor-sign working consists of merely drawing a sign, saying a magical spell of some sort, and letting it do its work. All that is needed is paper and pen. But this is a fairly advanced stage for most people. Some will find they have an innate knack for this sort of magic, while others may have the knack and then lose it along the way. This is because galdor-sign magic is an art, not a science. In the beginning of one's practice a bit more ritualism may be needed to focus and redirect the mind to do the work. This is as elaborate as such a ritual ever needs to be. The basic format of such a ritual is as follows:

1. Opening
2. Invoke Óðinn: pour red wine, give half to Oðinn in a pure state, and then mix wine and water, which you drink
3. Create the sign
4. Anchor/charge the sign
5. Break from the sign
6. Closing

The ritual space is large enough to hold a table and chair. Stand behind the chair. The table is arranged as shown in figure 9.1 on page 68. Here follows a detailed description of all ritual procedures.

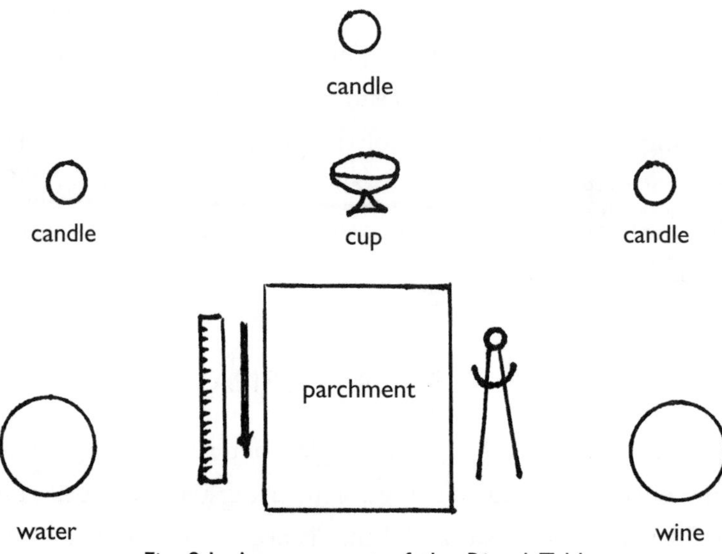


Fig. 9.1. Arrangement of the Ritual Table

### *1. Opening*

This is intended to sanctify the working space and protect the magician from outside interference.

According to traditional lore, Iceland is surrounded and protected by four "land spirits" (*landvættir*). These land spirits were first mentioned in Old Norse literature in the *Heimskringla* by Snorri Sturluson, where they are described as protecting the island from invasion. Today they are even depicted on several modern Icelandic coins. These same forms can be used to shield your personal working space from outside distractions or interference. This is not to imply that the forces being invoked are a danger but rather that other inner or outer patterns of thought or action may interfere with the concentrated will of the magician. The four guardian *landvættir* appear as follows: a dragon in the east, a large bird in the north, a bull in the west, and a mountain giant (*bergrisi*) with an iron bar in his hand in the south.

The following ritual can be used to shield the practitioner.

### ❄ Call to the *Landvættir*

Stand behind the table in the middle of the space you intend to sanctify. Face east and with arms uplifted in the ᛉ-rune posture and say:

"From the East swims the dragon, to the dread of my foes."

Then turn to the north and, in the same posture, say: "From the North flies the eagle, to give me insight."

Next, turn to the west and say: "From the West charges the bull, to give me might and main."

And finally, turn to the south and speak the formula: "From the South strides forth the rock-giant, to make me steadfast."

As you do each of these stations, visualize the entity in question coming forth from your center and going out to a place at the outer extreme of the space you are hallowing.

## *2. Invoke Óðinn*

Now sit down in the chair and light the three candles: first, the black one with the words "I am fed"; second, the red one with the words "I am shielded"; and third, the white one with the words "I am hallowed by the might and main of the strongest of spirits in Valhöll: Óðinn."

Now silently pour wine (grape juice may be substituted) into a glass, filling it halfway. Then pour an equal amount of spring water into the glass. Next, pour pure wine (or juice) into a sacrificial bowl as a gift to the All-Father (Óðinn). Now drink the mixture of water and wine. Contemplate your spirit rising up to meet that of Óðinn as an equal partner in the working of magic.

## *3. Create the Sign*

Now sit at your ritual table. Focus and concentrate your mind on the work at hand. Take your drawing tools and execute the sign as quickly and as skillfully as possible. Your consciousness should enter into the sign through your instrument as you draw or carve it. When a sign is well executed it can be *felt.* Speak any words that are to be uttered in the working upon completion of the sign as instructed.

### *4. Anchor/Charge the Sign*

Next, fix the sign in your mind by concentrating on its form. Enter into or become one with the sign in spirit. It should be visualized as existing in one or the other of the various matrices of meaning discussed below. It may be seen in three or more dimensions, or the runes that make up the sign may be clearly articulated in your mind. This process should be done quickly and requires practice through prior meditative work.

### *5. Break from the Sign*

After this step you should break your awareness away from the sign as completely as possible. The sign can be hidden or placed in a significant place away from your sight. The important thing is that the sign, on an inner level, is to be *released* to do its work. Continued attachment to your consciousness will only drag it back to you and away from the work it has been created to do.

### *6. Closing*

At the conclusion of your ritual, definitely end your work with a final gesture. This is done with a simple phrase and gesture. Those of a Christian persuasion will use the Paternoster in Latin. Most others will simply clasp their hands before them, lower their arms to a 45-degree angle imitative of the final ᛣ-rune, and say:

So shall it be!
*Svo skal það vera!*

## GUIDE TO SPECIAL INSTRUCTIONS

When instructions say that you should carry a sign "in the middle of your breast" or "on your head," two things can be meant. It can mean that you should carry the physical stave as written on parchment or paper in a pouch so that it hangs in front of your chest or under a hat or headgear. It also can mean that you are to visualize the sign in the midst of your body or head, for example. Both the physical and spiritual versions are valid, and either can be used. Practical experimentation can be your only true guide here.

## THE INNER NATURE OF GALDOR

Ultimately, the most powerful rituals are performed entirely in the mental, visualized manner that is free of external props or designs. The externals are always merely aids and mnemonic devices for the *inner* work. Working in an entirely abstract, inner manner will open the gate to the performance of galdor staves in your sleep, and in the final analysis this kind of work extends even into a post-mortem process. Many legends relate how galdor men of old had their books buried with them, which is a sign that they intended to take the magic with them and practice it even after death. In such a "performance" one sees the *galdra-myndir* in multiple dimensions as if in a space unfettered by the limits of the written page, and the rainbow bridge is crossed. This is the bridge between the objective view (in which you see the sign "out there") and the subjective view (in which you see yourself as an *embodiment* of the sign or existing or moving within the sign). These signs are devices for focusing and directing the mind in specific, effective patterns of thought. They are images of the mind and will and the relationship of these to the universe. This universe is not only the environment in which events take place but also includes the collective and individual psyches of other individuals.

On an experimental level the magician can undertake simple workings with sign magic as a way to test for effectiveness and also to discover the characteristic functions of certain features of the signs. Just drawing a sign on a piece of paper with full inner focus—along with the obligatory break with your mental attachment to the sign to allow it to work on its own—can yield surprising results. Keep such experiments to harmless modulations in the environment of the minds of others. Such experiments seem to work best on small groups of people; for example, attracting business to a store or keeping people away for short periods of time. You should allow yourself to be free to play with forms and record your results. Ultimately, it will be found that different signs work differently with and for different people.

## AIMS OF GALDOR

Once the grammar of the galdor staves and galdor signs has been mastered—no easy feat, it must be admitted—the practitioner is free to create his or her own signs to effect things magically. It will become like carrying on a conversation with the world order. As wisdom is gained it will be learned just what communications the world is open to and which ones it is not open to. Learn to speak to a receptive world. In general the Father of Magic is your friend and wants to help you in your endeavors. But more than anything he wants to teach you to be wise.

The aims of galdor-sign magic are virtually limitless, but the following list represents many of the more common uses, in no particular order.

- discovery
- strength
- safety
- luck
- influence over others
- safe journey
- acquisition of love/sex
- acquisition of money
- success in business
- wisdom
- guidance
- safe crossing of barriers
- gaining access to hidden knowledge

- finding one's way in unknown territory
- courage
- healing sickness
- opposing enemies
- identifying who has wronged you

## INTERPRETATION AND CONSTRUCTION OF SIGNS

With galdor signs the magician can map and remap reality in conformity with the will. The most powerful act of magic and the greatest form of "prayer" is that which is given geometrical reality (as a unique stave) in harmony with a verbal message (the corresponding spell) and hidden in the realm of the secret will—deep and inaccessible to the conscious mind—but inexorably linked to the realm out of which events emerge.

It can be said that there are three distinct types of magical figures used in the kind of Icelandic magic contained in black books of the kind you now possess. These are:

1. *ægishjálmar* (helms of awe)
2. *galdramyndir* (magical signs)
3. *galdrastafir* (magical staves)

The latter two are usually not distinguished in later times, although the terminology itself appears to indicate that the *galdramyndir* were originally more free-form, whereas the *galdrastafir* were generated from runes, magical letters (*galdraletur*), and especially from bindrunes (*bandrúnar*). To understand the runes and the much less well-known tradition of "magical letters" found in historical manuals of magic in Iceland, we have included lists of them in appendices A and C.

## ÆGISHJÁLMAR

The simplest magical sign in Icelandic magic is the basic *ægishjálmur*, or "helm of awe."

Fig. 9.2. Simple ægishjálmur

The name of this figure has been associated with the "serpent power" present in the body of humans, which is mythically linked to the dragon or serpent Fáfnir, slain by the great hero Sigurd. This myth is recounted in the *Eddas* as well as in the *Völsunga Saga*. Historical magical books such as the *Galdrabók* show that the sign is closely associated with the area of the forehead between the eyes of a human being.

The fact that this figure is called a "helm"—more literally, a "covering"—indicates that in fact its power is intended to overlay or subsume the reality over which it is cast by the will and design of the magician. This is done at two different levels: subjectively or objectively. When used subjectively, this means that the power is cast over the magician in workings of self-transformation. Here we are reminded that the man or giant Fáfnir actually *transformed* himself into a serpent with the ægishjálmur's power. When extended objectively, this means that the power is cast over the world or environment surrounding the magician in workings of sorcery. What makes the helm of awe an especially powerful "map of magic" is that it connects the subjective and objective universes in a synthetic way, which gives the inner will of the magician a high level of influence over the objective universe, because both realms are clearly seen as parts of the same whole.

The entire visible plane, or two-dimensional field, onto which the helm of awe is drawn or cast represents the whole universe. Within this greater plane there is a circular zone that represents the subjective universe of the magician: his soul and mind, and their contents. At the very core of the circle is the self of the magician, the source of the magical casting itself. Alternatively, the core can be made to represent the object, or aim, of the magic. This can be "mapped" in the manner shown in figure 9.3.

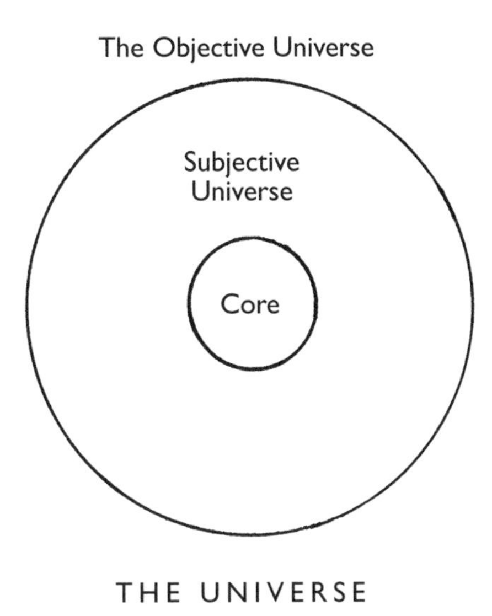


Fig. 9.3. Zones of mapping for some magical signs

The zones of the *ægishjálmur* can be further refined, but we will leave this up to more empirical results of magical experimentation within the tradition. It is hoped that a community of students and teachers of this kind of magic will develop in the years to come.

In casting a helm of awe the magician is to imagine the arms of the sign as currents of force emitting from the core of his being and flowing both outwardly and inwardly—being projected forcefully, remaining steady, being received forcefully or being blocked, redirected, or circulated as the sign determines. Again, the key is that the sign is *not two-dimensional,* but it exists on *at least four dimensions.* Begin by seeing and feeling the sign as a three-dimensional figure—as existing in a sphere. The three-dimensional model of Yggdrasill, the Germanic world tree that vertically and horizontally encompasses the many worlds of the universe, is a good conceptual place to start. The typical eight-armed *ægishjálmur* is really a reference to the four cardinal directions and the four vertical worlds along an axis both above and below the subject as conceived of anywhere in space. The two inner worlds on the vertical axis are above and below the subject, but the outer two on the vertical pole are actually in another dimension of time and space: these correspond to the realm from which events originate and the realm where transformations are made.

Obviously the number of arms on a helm gives an indication of the way in which magical space is being modeled: typically the helms have eight, six, or four arms. Eight arms refer to the eight divisions of the sky and earth (the *ættir*); six arms refer to the four cardinal points and a vertical axis; while four arms refer to the cardinal points of the mundane universe. However, many more configurations are possible.

According to the zone-mapping model shown in figure 9.3 on page 75, the closer a symbol is to the center of the map, the closer it is to the middle of the subjective universe: either that of the magician or, alternatively, that of the object of his or her operation. In the multidimensional philosophy implied by galdor-sign magic, these are often *temporarily* seen as being one and the same. The farther out from the center that a symbol or feature is on the sign, the more it is reaching into the objective universe around the subject.

An example of a more complex helm of awe appears in figure 9.4. This shows a sign with a strong fortress of protection around the middle of the subjective center while insulating the inner and outer worlds from one another and projecting a fierce stance toward the outer world, which says that the subject casting the helm should be approached only with trepidation. This is a typical message sent by many helms of awe.

When charging or vivifying a helm of awe in a magical working, magicians are to visualize themselves at the center of the figure, their souls configured by the geometry of the inner part of the sign while their

Fig. 9.4. A helm of awe

wills are powerfully projected out through the arms of the sign. The power is modified, modulated, and shaped according to the nature of the terminal figures. These can either thrust outward into the universe surrounding the magician or, alternatively, put up shields around the magician. Experiment empirically with the specific shapes of the symbols and use what feels right for you at the time. Being overly prescriptive in a dogmatic way about these matters leads to diminished effectiveness.

## *GALDRAMYNDIR*

The magical signs or images called *galdramyndir* are those that have their origins in abstract or hidden keys other than runes. Technically speaking, the term *galdrastafur* ("magical stave") can be reserved for those signs that have their origins in rune-stave shapes (see fig. 9.5 on p. 78).

One glance at a book of Icelandic magic will give the viewer the impression of many wild and entirely unintelligible signs. To some extent these signs can be interpreted, but it is only to a limited extent because fundamental to their construction and execution is the idea that there is a synthesis of rule-bound regularity or predictability and a subjective, creative whimsy. This latter element is important to the idea of hiding the meaning of the sign—even from the conscious mind of the one who created it!

Icelandic magical signs are represented in the realm of two dimensions, most often on a flat piece of paper or parchment or carved on a flat piece of wood. However, the signs are in fact multidimensional. The key to charging them is to see them in multidimensions. Using your spatial imagination, make them "pop" off the page. When this happens, you have made contact with the spirit of the sign.

Other extra-dimensional aspects of signs include the alchemy of the senses: signs can appear as *visual* graphic models in space, but they can be endowed with qualities of *sound* as well.

As we saw in chapter 5, one of the elements of the southern Mediterranean tradition that found a quick and easy home in the North was the use of so-called magical squares. The famous *sator*-square is found in several runic inscriptions from all over Scandinavia in the Middle Ages. It is utilized in a very practical way. In line with this, it seems logical that a numerical/runic square of sixteen segments would also find a useful place in the practice of Icelandic galdor-sign magic.

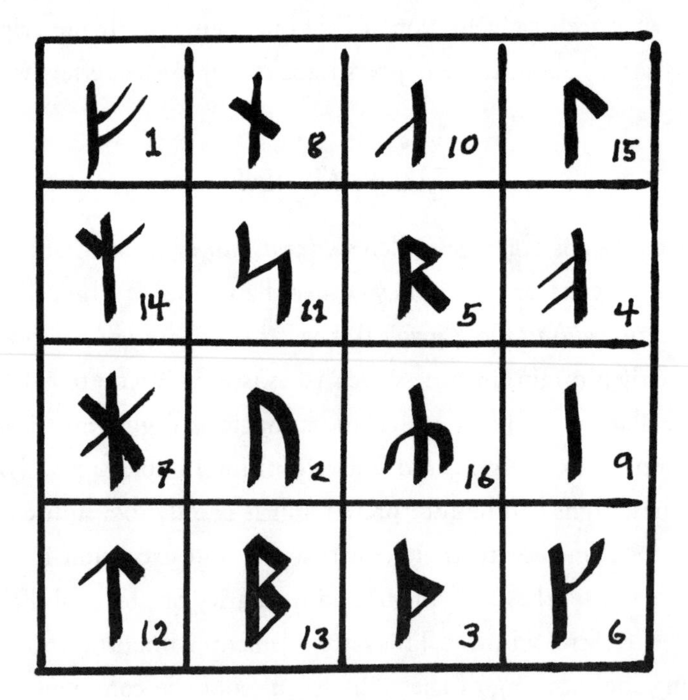


Fig. 9.5. A sixteenfold magical square with numbers and runes

This particular square is used as a powerful tool both to analyze certain preexisting signs found in the traditional record and to create meaningful new signs of your own. One of the important esoteric principles for working galdor-sign magic is that of *hiding* the obvious meaning of a sign by the use of such tools. By hiding the meaning (even from the conscious mind of the operator) the magical effects can work more freely and quickly in the worlds beyond Midgard—beyond the realm of the five senses and three dimensions that constantly feed this world with events.

We can create an apparently abstract magical sign by connecting the runes that make up a name (of Óðinn, for example) or a concept (translated into Old Norse) in such a way that a geometrical figure emerges, which, in reality, is a "magical runic signature" of the word in question.

The first step in creating a magical sign based on an Old Norse name or word is to transliterate the word into runes. By way of example, we will transliterate the Odinic nickname Sig-Týr (Victory God) into runes following the rules given in appendix A. Doing this, we come up with ᛊᛁᚴᛏᚢᚱ.

Now we take the sixteen-rune grid and trace the name through the runes and come up with the shape shown in figure 9.6. This shape is

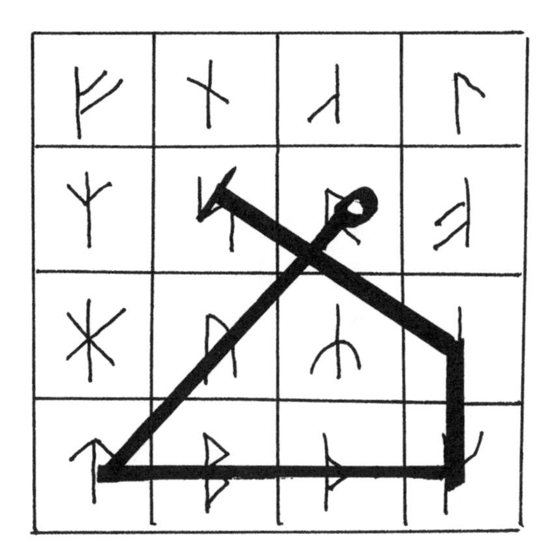

Fig. 9.6. The raw signature of ᛊᛁᚴᛏᚢᚱ

Fig. 9.7. The finished signature of ᛊᛁᚴᛏᚢᚱ

then further stylized and provided with flourishes for magico-esthetic reasons. The final shape is shown in figure 9.7.

## *GALDRASTAFIR*

Many galdor staves begin as runic symbols that make up words or names in Old Norse. Sometimes these runes are themselves stylized to conceal their identity from even those versed in rune lore. At other times they are combined into so-called bindrunes or runic monograms, which are often then further stylized according to aesthetic and magical intent. Concealing the runes and their outer meaning from the conscious mind seems to have been a prime motive of the ancient practitioners of galdor-stave magic.

Of course, everything that has been said thus far about traditional signs leads the practitioner to knowledge of how to construct new signs with the correct magical meaning for given operations.

In my 1992 book, *Northern Magic,* written under the name Edred Thorsson, I first discussed the semiotics of *galdrastafir.* The specifics of the lines making up the signs constitute the metaphysical "words" in this magical language, while certain symbolic matrices make up its hidden "grammar." It could therefore be said that the kinds of magical signs shown in the Gray-Skin section of this book provide a geometry of the will. Others have remarked that the galdor signs appear to be akin to the "circuit boards of consciousness." Altering the circuits causes alterations to occur in the mind and/or in the universe of events.

Magical signs were first uncovered by ancient magicians using a method of trial and error. When they hit upon signs that worked for them, they recorded them in their books and made notes about their effectiveness. Such effective signs were then used by subsequent generations, and they became traditional. There is no reason why current galdor practitioners cannot do the same thing. However, for the sake of your own rate of success it is recommended that you stick with some traditional signs for the beginning phases of your work. You have to get through the beginning before you can reach the middle and go beyond.

When converted to magical signs, the names of Óðinn shown in appendix C can be used for a wide variety of operative aims. The interpretations of these names suggest a wide range of such aims: if one wants inspiration, use Óðinn; if one wants success in business, use Farmatýr; if one wants a wish fulfilled, use Óski; and so on. In chapter 4, I showed how names of Óðinn were used in history for exactly this purpose and in exactly this way. This form of magic is very ancient and obviously long in use in Iceland before it was atavistically "rediscovered" by modern magicians such as Austin Osman Spare.

How are these names to be transformed into magical signs? Here there is a science and there is an art. The science indicates that there is a definite mode of transliterating the names into runes of the Younger Futþąrk. To do this, follow the rules provided in appendix A of this book. The process of learning how to do the transliterations is actually a dimension of magical preparation. If someone else was to do it for you, the magic would not be as effective.

The names of Óðinn in runic form already constitute a magical avenue for the activation of the power of the name for operative purposes. These names in runic form can have the indicated effect and can be written, carved, or scratched in ritual format to effect the operation.

However, for the greatest potency, to "key" the working at the deepest levels, these runic formulas should be converted into *galdrastafir.* This is where the artistic aspect comes in. The names should be converted to runes according to certain rules as indicated, but they are combined into bindrune-based magical signs according to the aesthetic sense of the magician. The aim of the operation also plays a part: if the operation seeks harmony and goodwill, symmetry and grace may be your guiding principle, but if destruction or chaos is your aim, then perhaps the resulting magical sign should reflect this spirit.

Besides names of Óðinn, Old Norse words that express a specific magical aim can be transliterated into runes and combined into bindrunes in the same fashion to similar effect. For example, if someone wants peaceful relations with others, the Icelandic word *friður* (or its earlier Old Norse form, *friðr*), meaning "peace," could be transliterated according to the rules in appendix A, rendering ᚠᚱᛁᚦᚢᛦ or ᚠᚱᛁᚦᛦ. Then this word is turned into a bindrune and stylized as shown in figure 9.8.

Fig. 9.8. Galdor stave based on the Old Norse word *friðr*

# PART TWO

# *Gray-Skin*

# INTRODUCTION TO THE WORKINGS

What follows is the Gray-Skin proper. The first part of this book was an introduction to the history, theory, and practical principles of Icelandic galdor-stave magic. The second part is a unique book of magic in the traditional Icelandic form. This whole book is not part of a program of any specific magical order or school, although it is a product of work done in the Rune-Gild from about 1981 to the present. The work really belongs to anyone who grasps its principles and makes the grammar of the metalanguage work for himself or herself. This form of magic is very close to pure art, and there will be those with greater or lesser degrees of talent in this art. The author is interested in hearing from successful practitioners of the system. Most of my own success with the system has come from using it in moments of dire need, and for the sake of discovering unknown, yet traditional, aspects of the system itself. It should be noted that the texts in what follows are sometimes not literal translations of the original Icelandic texts but have been adapted for current use and effectiveness. Literal translations can be found in the various scholarly books included in the bibliography.

The practical section of this book, chapter 9, gives detailed instructions on how to work with these signs and formulas. As a general rule the content of the workings below is inserted in the operative part of the ritual format outlined in chapter 9. The texts below show the working-specific data to be employed for certain definite aims. Occasionally the instructions call for actions to be performed "in the field" and not in your ritual space. These workings are for the most part historical or traditional examples of galdor-stave magic. This is the best way to learn. They are intended as training for more original work once the grammar of the system is to some extent mastered. The current galdor man or galdor woman is as free now as the Icelandic magicians of old were to create original signs and staves based on the principles outlined in chapter 9 of this book. Those workings will probably be found to be even more effective than the historical examples. Remember that this form of magic was first and foremost pragmatic, and to be true to its spirit the current practitioner should be innovative rather than hidebound with respect to the tradition.

Pages have been intentionally left blank at the end of the book (pp. 133–38) for you to inscribe your most successful workings in the traditional fashion. This will make the book truly your own.

In general the following workings have been grouped according to theme and type. The higher and more spiritual kinds of workings come first, followed by more basic motivations. The pragmatic world of Icelandic galdor-stave magic takes all aspects of human life into account. The needs of humanity are many and the gods of Heaven, Hell, and Valhöll are all brought to bear.

Although this book is not intended as a scholarly tome, readers today are often curious about the origins and sources of things. For this reason each of the workings below has been referenced to the original Icelandic manuscript or edited and published work from which it came. Some workings have been adapted or modified for current usage, and there are a few that have been recorded in this book for the first time. Each of the newer workings has been tested and has been shown to be effective.

## I. WISDOM

These workings lead the practitioner to insight, greater knowledge, discovery of the unknown, and generally open the soul to the workings of wisdom.

### 1 ❄ To Awaken Yourself to a Sense of Mystery and Wonder

Draw this sign with white or silver ink on black paper at midnight on the Spring Equinox. Hide the sign in a wooden box. This spell works over a lifetime.

### 2 ❄ For Insight into Things beyond the Earthly Realm

Write this stave with red ink on white paper. Put it in a wooden box or carry it with you in your left breast pocket, and insight into heavenly things will come to you.

### 3 ❄ To Link Yourself with the Power and Knowledge of Your Soul

To bind yourself fast to the power of your own soul, draw these staves on parchment and keep them with you always.

### 4 ❄ To Know the Unknown

To be able to understand and analyze hidden things and patterns of manifestation, draw this stave and keep it in your room in a secret location.

### 5 ❄ Discovering the Unknown (Lbs 2413 8vo 100)

If you desire to know what is concealed from the common folk, carve these staves on brass with a steel instrument and put it near your ear and sleep and you will experience [*reyna*] it.

### 6 ❄ Concealment (Lbs 2413 8vo 73)

If you want to hide something so it will not be found, carve this stave with your eating knife and the object in question will not be found; read the Paternoster.

### 7 ❄ For Gaining Inspiration

Write this stave on parchment in red ink. Conceal it in a place high up in your room. Inspiration will come.

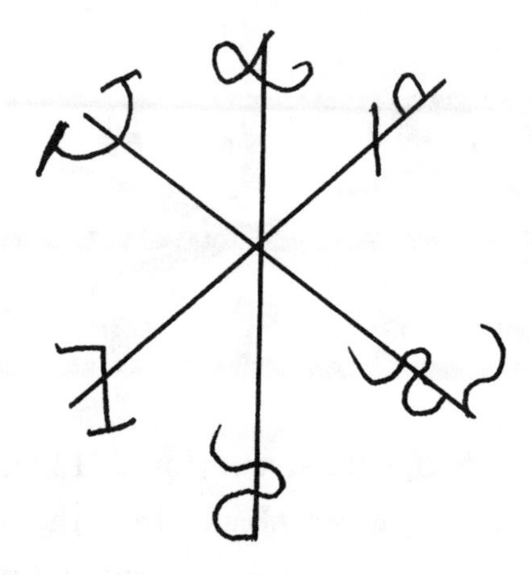

### 8 ❄ Wayfinder (Davíðsson XXX)

If this sign, called the *Vegvísir* (way shower), is carried, one will never lose one's way in storms or bad weather, even when the way is not known. It also helps one find one's way in life.

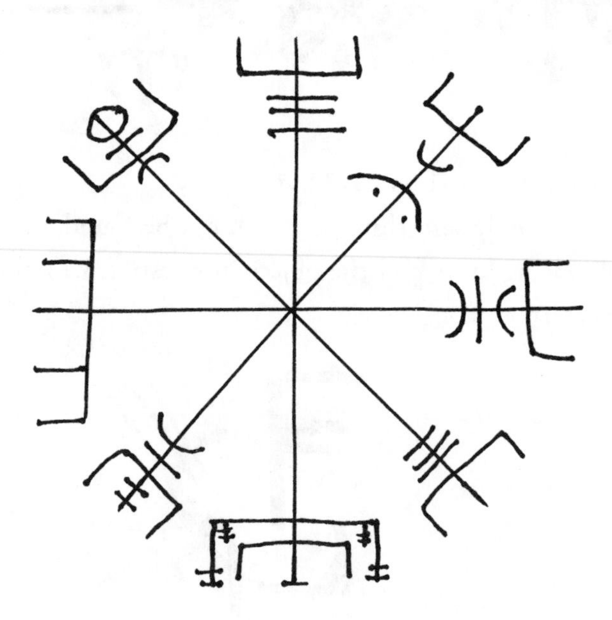

### 9 ❄ Thief-Detective (*Galdrabók* 33)

For theft: Carve these staves on the bottom of a bowl made of ash wood and put water in it and grind *millefolium** in the water and say: "This I ask by the herb's power and the greatness of the stave, that the shade of the one who has stolen may be seen in the water." And carve these names with runes on parchment and keep the parchment on your person: Óðinn, Loki, Frey[r], Baldur, Njörður, Týr, Birgir, Hœnir, Freyja, Gefun, Gusta, and all those who dwell in Valhöll and have dwelt there from the beginning of the world, provide me with the power so that what has been stolen will be returned, and the thief will be found out.

### 10 ❄ Sitting-Out Stave (Skuggi's *Galdra-Skræða,* 77)

Icelandic tradition knows of a ritual of seeking knowledge from extrahuman sources, variously characterized as "the dead," "elves," "trolls," and "devils." These entities are encountered by sitting out all night at a crossroad. Ideally there should be cemeteries at some point down each

*The herbological element in this spell is twofold: (1) ash wood and (2) *millefolium* (yarrow, *Achillea millefolium*). In the manuscript the Latin word *millefolium* is written *mellifolium.* Ash is of well-known properties in Germanic myth and magic. Here it may signify the ability to make contact with other worlds. Yarrow, which was either ground up or its flowers made into an essential oil to be mixed with water, also is thought to have tremendous powers for making contact with "the other side," the unconscious. Not only did the ancient Chinese know of this (see the I-Ching literature), but it was also well known among the Indo-Europeans as a divinatory tool. In later times it was widely thought to be connected to "the Evil One" and was popularly called the "Devil's Nettle" and "Bad Man's Plaything"; it was used in magical rites. Its common name in Icelandic is *vallhumall* (see Sæmundsson, *Galdrar á Íslandi,* 374).

of the four roads. The all-night vigil can be rewarded by the "appearance" of an entity that will impart some secret information. Generally the practitioner should be open to receive what the entity is willing to communicate and not try to force some predetermined result. The twentieth-century Icelandic magician known as Skuggi provided the following sign used by practitioners of "sitting out" to enhance the chances of success with this kind of working.

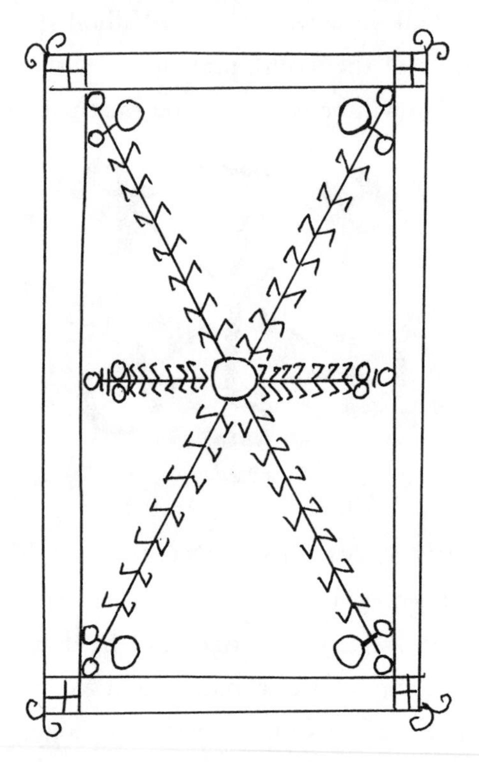

## II. POWER

Many magical formulas show the way to gain power of some sort. This can come in many forms, sometimes directly, sometimes indirectly.

### 1 ❄ Winning Struggles of all Kinds (Jón Árnason, I, 438)

To win any and all internal struggles with your own nature, or in conflicts with others, draw these staves and place *Gapaldur* under the heel of your right foot and *Ginfaxi* under the toe of your left foot, and say:

| | |
|---|---|
| *Gapaldur undir hæli,* | *Gapaldur under my heel,* |
| *Ginfaxi undir tá,* | *Ginfaxi under my toe,* |
| *stattu hjá mér, fjandi,* | *stand by me, my fiend,* |
| *ví nú liggur mér á!* | *for now I've got to get going!* |

### 2 ❄ Victory (Jón Árnason, I, 438)

Draw this helm of awe on a disk of lead and press it to your forehead between your eyebrows and say:

| | |
|---|---|
| *Ægishjálm er ég ber* | *I bear the helm of awe* |
| *milli brúna mér!* | *between my brows!* |

You will have victory in every struggle: the powerful will love you and

your enemies will be struck with terror. Victory is assured.

### 3 ❄ To Win a Debate (Lbs 2413 8vo 69)

Write this stave with your saliva while you are fasting and put it under your left arm if you don't want anyone to get the better of you in a debate or argument.

### 4 ❄ *Herzlustafir* (strengthening staves) (Davíðsson XXXIV)

Make this double-sided stave and wear it on the left side of your chest to strengthen your courage and resolve.

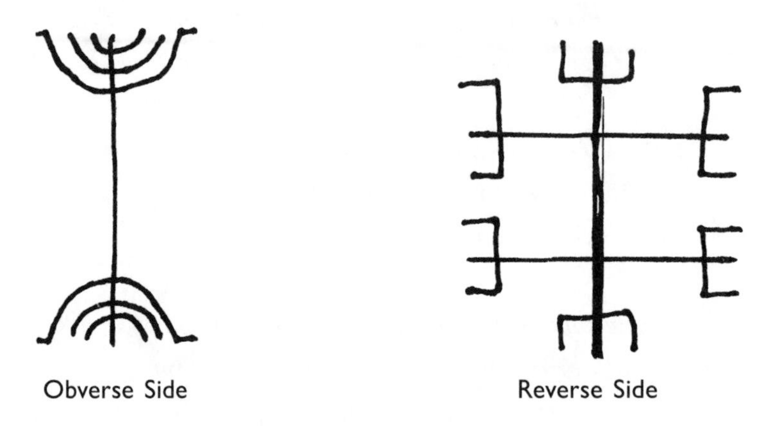

Obverse Side Reverse Side

## III. PROTECTION

People need protection from all sorts of dangers, some from the environment and some from the malice of others. Galdor-stave magic addresses all these concerns.

### 1 ❄ Return to Sender (Davíðsson XXXVII)

Have this sign on leather on the front of your chest if you want to send back any harmful message to the one who sent it to you.

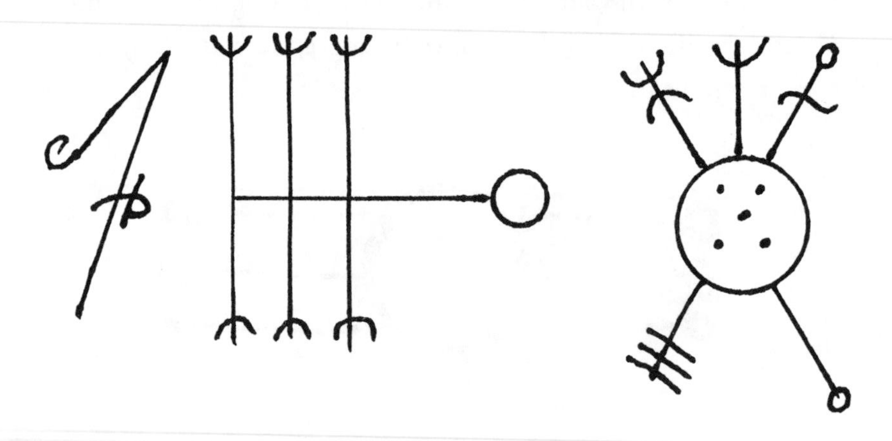

### 2 ❄ Protection from Embarrassment (Davíðsson XXXVIII)

So that you will remain free of any shame or embarrassment, no matter what or who you encounter. Using spittle, make this sign on your forehead with the ring finger of your right hand.

### 3 ❄ A Washing Verse: To Wash Away Ill Will and Negativity (Jón Árnason, I, 439)

To ward off the effects of negative thoughts of others and to prevent harm by the thoughts or actions of other people, wash your face in cold spring water and recite the following verse.

| | |
|---|---|
| *Fjón þvær ég af mér* | *I wash the hate from me* |
| *fjanda minna* | *of my enemies* |
| *rann ok reiði* | *(and the) robbery and wrath* |
| *ríkra manna!* | *of powerful men!* |

### 4 ❄ Sorcery Prevention (Lbs 2413 8vo 112)

Draw this stave on parchment with black ink. Keep it near you.

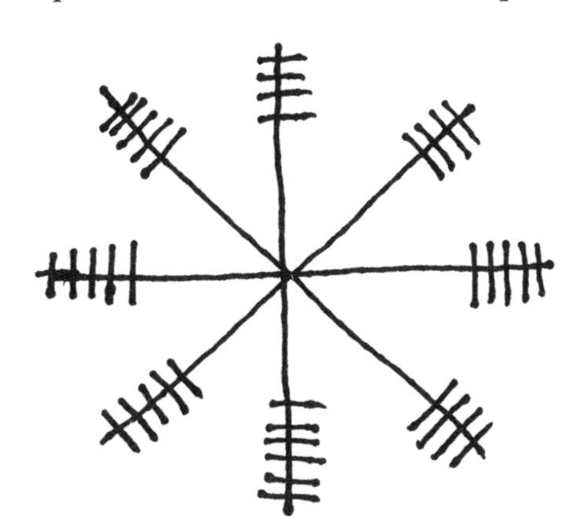

### 5 ❄ Against Foreboding When You Go into the Darkness (Davíðsson XXXIX)

Carve these signs on an oak stave and wear it under your left arm. This is good for both literal darkness and for dark periods in life.

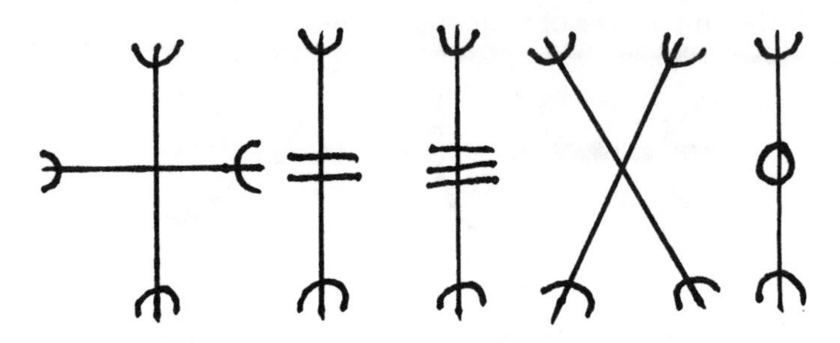

### 6 ❄ Against All Witchery (Davíðsson XXXV)

Write this sign on parchment and have it in your right hand against all witchery and any fear of witchery.

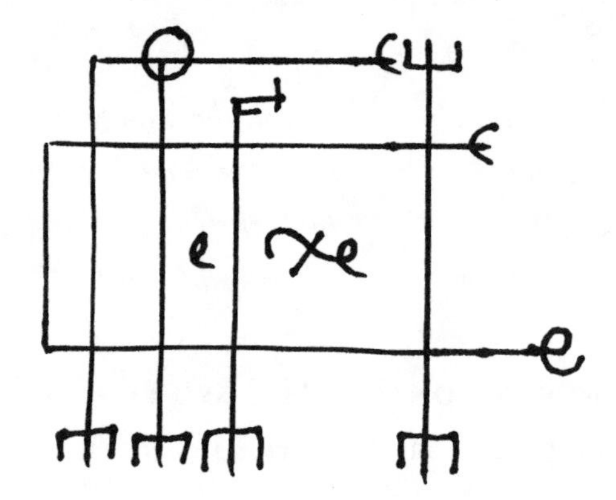

## IV. CONTROL

Magic is often concerned with the concept of control. This could be self-control, or the control of the environment or other people.

### 1 ❄ To Calm Anger (*Galdrabók* 41)

To calm all anger make this stave on your forehead with the index finger of your left hand and say: "It is the helm of awe, which I bear between my eyes. Let the anger melt, let the strife stop. May every man rejoice in me as Mary rejoiced in her blessed son when she found him on the victory rock. In the name of the Father and Son and Holy Spirit."

And read:

*Ølvir, Óðinn, Illi,**
*everything may your will bewilder.*
*May God himself with mastery,*
*send love between us.*

### 2 ❄ To Gain the Favor of Powerful Persons (*Galdrabók* 17)

You should write it on parchment and have it on your person generally, and powerful people will like you very much.

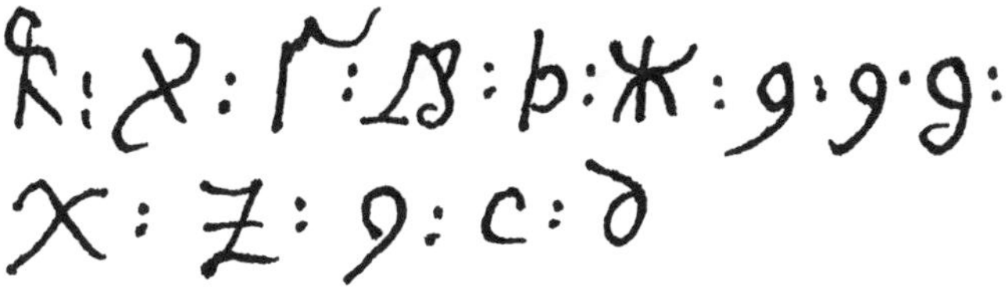

### 3 ❄ To Cause Fear in an Enemy (*Galdrabók* 9)

If you want your enemies to be afraid of you when they see you, then

*This threefold Odinic invocation includes the name Óðinn beside *Illi,* "the Evil One," which may have been an old name for Óðinn, because he was called *Bölverkr,* "Evil Worker," and was called "the father of all evil" in pagan times. Ølvir is interesting. It is our name "Oliver" and comes from Proto-Germanic *Alawīhaz,* "the All-Holy-One." This is similar in meaning to the name "Wīhaz" (ON *Vé*), the third name in the primal threefold Odinic formulation of Oðinn, Vili, and Vé.

carve these staves on a piece of oak wood and wear it in the middle of your chest, and see to it that you see them before they see you.

### 4 ❄ Against the Ill Will of Powerful Persons (*Galdrabók* 26)

Make the helm of awe between your eyes. Then read the following formula three times down into your cupped hands filled with spring water. Read a Paternoster in Latin at the conclusion of each reading.

"I wash my enemies away from me along with the thievery and anger of powerful persons, so that they may now approach me with good cheer and look into my eyes laughingly. I enforce affection with my hand, I discharge monetary debts, I discharge the accusations of the most powerful persons. Let God see me, and let every man look upon me, with eyes of bliss. I bear the helm of awe between my brows. May the world and the land provide me with many friends."

### 5 ❄ To Calm the Anger of an Enemy (Davíðsson, Kreddur 27)

He should go to some water and before a raven flies over it (that is, before dawn) he should hold his hands in the water for a while and then make the following runes on his forehead with the fourth finger of the right hand and afterward not wash himself off.

### 6 ❄ To Have Success in a Meeting (Davíðsson IV)

Have this sign on gray paper under your left arm when you are talking to somebody and you will have success with them.

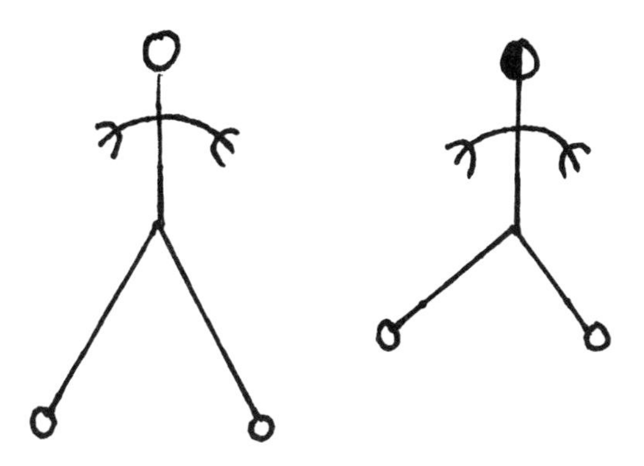

### 7 ❄ *Dúnfaxi* (Down Mane)—To Win a Law Case (Davíðsson VII)

If you want to win a law case, carry this sign with you, if you believe in it. It is called *Dúnfaxi.* Carve the sign on a piece of oak wood and hide it on your person before you go to where the trial is to be held.

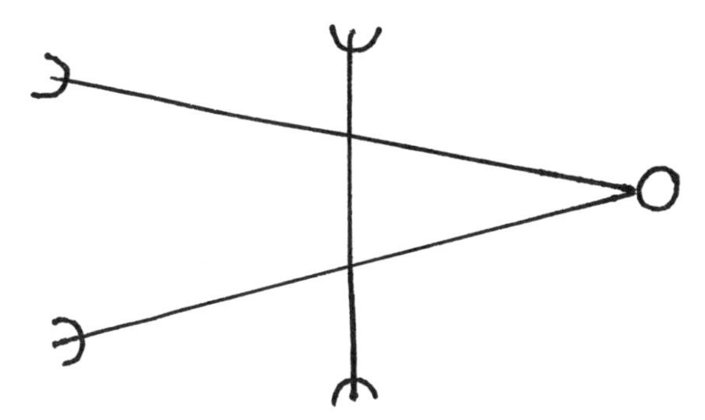

### 8 ❄ The Silencer (*Galdrabók* 43)

If you don't want someone to talk about you, take this stave, *Homa,** and visualize it infusing the person's entire being; he or she will not be

*Probably the name of a magical sign. It is unclear whether the two staves referred to here correspond to the stave represented in the manuscript. *Homa* perhaps refers to an image of the Iranian tree of life (and the ancient sacred and intoxicating drink *haoma* cognate to the Sanskrit *soma*). It is certainly possible that the *galdrastafur* represented here is a highly stylized version of such a treelike sign.

able to reveal anything. Also have this stave at your breast for as long as you require discretion.

To charge the signs say: "For this help me all the gods: Þórr, Óðinn, Frigg, Freyja, Satan, Beelzebub, and all those who inhabit Valhöll. In your mightiest name: Óðinn!"

## V. PROSPERITY

One of the most abiding motives for magicians throughout history has been the gaining of prosperity. The Icelandic approach is very pragmatic and realistic. It presupposes that the individual is actually working toward prosperity but just needs a bit of help to get some advantage.

### 1 ❄ Deal-Closer (*Kaupaloki*) (Davíðsson III)

Draw this stave on parchment and carry it in the center of your chest and you will have success in both buying and selling.

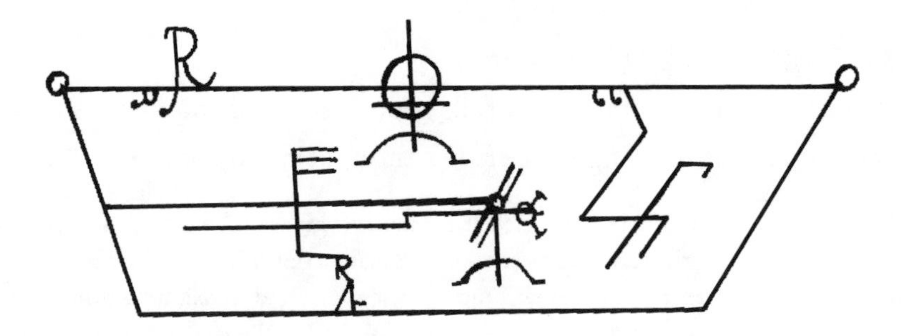

### 2 ❄ To Have Success in Business (Lbs 2413 8vo 32)

Write this stave on parchment or carve it into oak wood. Keep this stave in your hand when doing business. You will have success.

### 3 ❄ Another *Kaupaloki* (Davíðsson VIII)

Cut this sign on a piece of beech wood or draw it on parchment and you will have success in business deals.

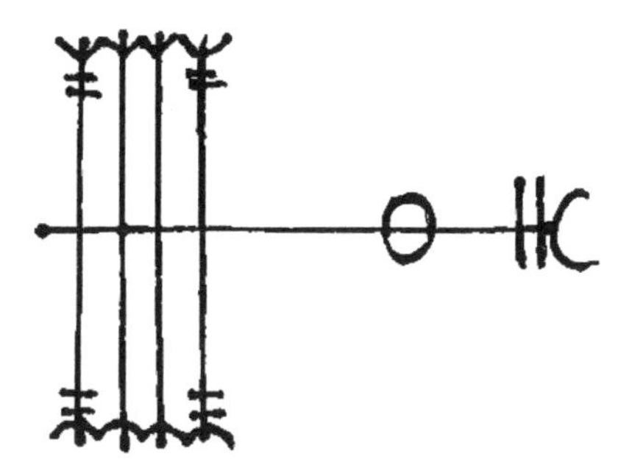

## VI. LOVE

One of the other abiding interests of magicians historically has been the acquisition of lovers. The galdor-stave magic of the Icelanders is rich in such operations.

### 1 ❄ Luck in Love (*Galdrabók* 8)

While fasting, make this helm of awe with your spittle in the palm of your right hand when you greet the person whom you want to have.

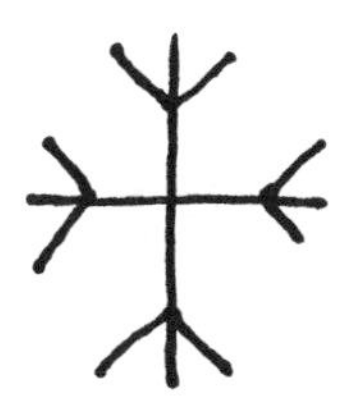

### 2 ❄ To Enchant a Woman and Win Her Love (*Galdrabók* 34)

If you want to enchant a woman so that she can find her way to no one except you, make a hole in the ground where she walks over it and put in etin-spear blood [semen] and draw a ring around the hole and carve her name and these staves: mold-*þurs* [ᚦ] and *maður* [ᛉ] inverted three-fold, that is, ᛦᛦᛦ, *bjarkan* [ᛒ], *nauð* [ᚾ], *homa,* and *gapaldur,* and read the following conjuration.

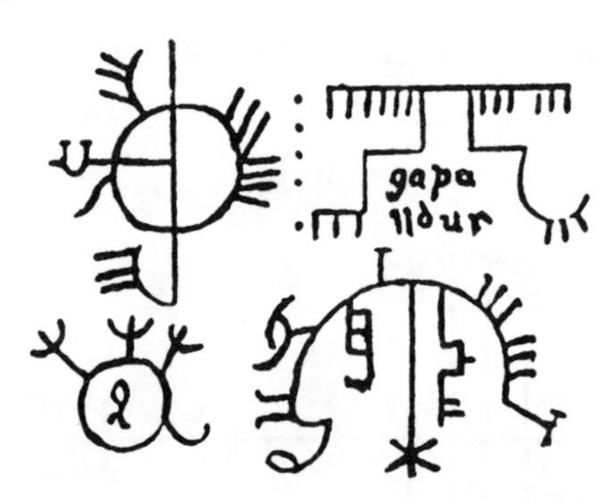


"I look at you and you feel love and affection for me with all your heart. You can't sit anywhere, nor stand to be anywhere without loving me. This I ask of Óðinn and of all those who know how to read women runes: that you can neither endure nor thrive unless you love me with all your heart. So it will be as if you were burning in your bones and even more so in your fleshly parts. It will be allotted to you to be unmarried unless you love me, you shall freeze in your feet, and never get honor or happiness. You'll sit as if burning, your hair falling out, your clothes torn asunder, unless you want to have me, you easygoing woman."

### 3 ❄ To Win the Love of a Person (*Galdrabók* 15)

You should write this on parchment and have it with you always, and people will love you very much.

## VII. RECEPTION OF LUCK AND RELEASE OF BLESSINGS

Because of the basic technique of galdor-stave magic, perhaps its strongest channel of effectiveness lies in the idea of becoming receptive to the inflow of power and/or meaning that leads to the reception of good influences.

### 1 ❄ The Luck Knot (Lbs 2413 8vo 141/142)

This is a man's luck knot (*Heillahnútur*). It should be drawn on parchment or carved on metal and carried on your person at all times to ensure good luck.

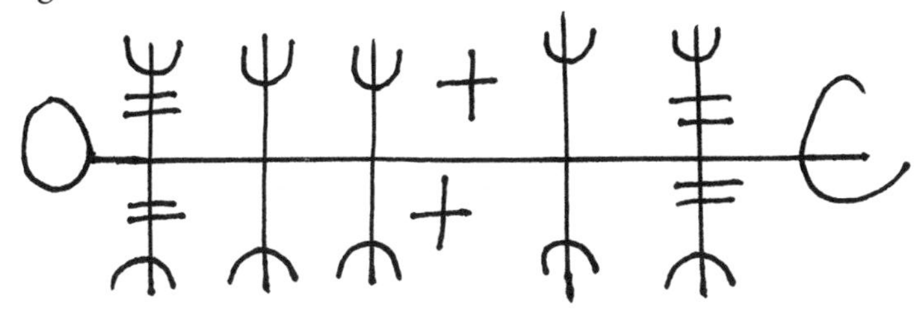

### 2 ❄ *Lukkustafir* (luck staves) (Davíðsson XXV)

Whoever carries these signs with him will meet with no bad luck, neither on sea nor on land.

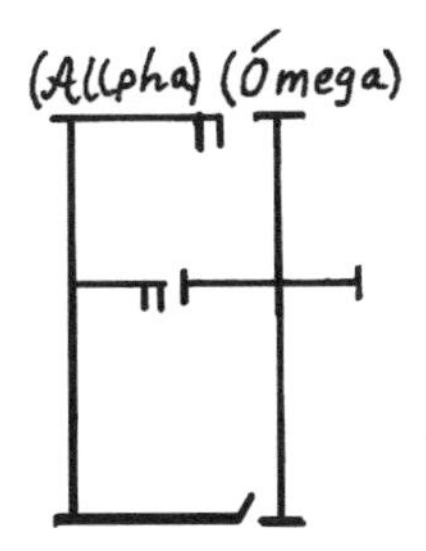


### 3 ❄ To Get Your Wish (Lbs 2413 8vo 27)

To get what you ask for, carve this stave on oak.

### 4 ❄ Release (Lbs 2413 8vo 115)

The following is called the SATOR verse. It is to be written and then read in every possible permutation. It is used to release things that are stuck and is good for everything from birthing children to bringing events to fruition in the world. Read the Paternoster in Latin afterward.

| S | A | T | O | R |
|---|---|---|---|---|
| A | R | E | P | O |
| T | E | N | E | T |
| O | P | E | R | A |
| R | O | T | A | S |

### 5 ❄ To Get Things to Turn Out as You Wish (Skuggi's *Galdra-Skræða* 19)

If you want to gain your petition of boon, draw this stave in your left palm.

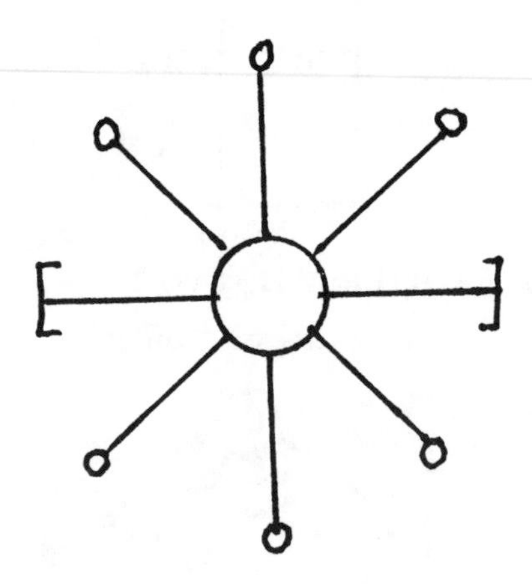

### 6 ❄ Good Luck (Skuggi's *Galdra-Skræða* 23)

This is a luck ring (*Lukkuhringur*). Draw this stave for good fortune; it works against any and all ill thoughts.

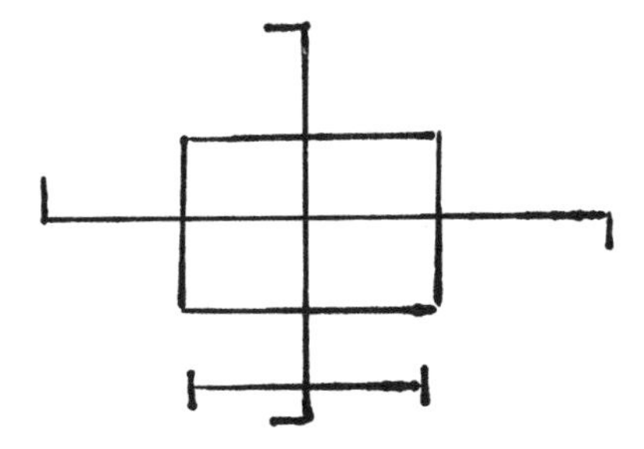

### 7 ❄ To Acquire the Object You Crave (Lbs 2413 8vo 34)

Carve this stave in lead and have it in your hand, whichever one you want. Carve it with your food knife and read this verse: *Da nobis Hodied dim: timi ej Petoribus Haftrus men Inducas.**

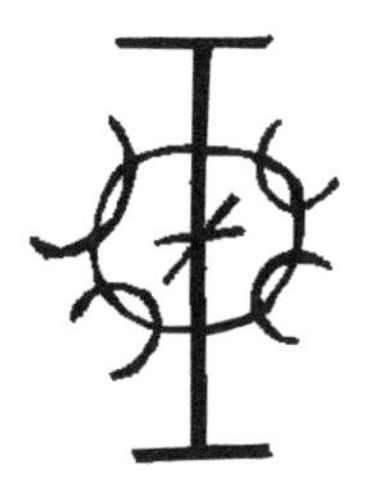

### 8 ❄ To Get Back What Was Stolen (Lbs 2413 8vo 131)

Carve this stave on an oak branch and hold it in your right hand and do this when the moon is one night old on Sunday, and sleep with it under your head. What has been stolen, or something of equal value, will be returned.

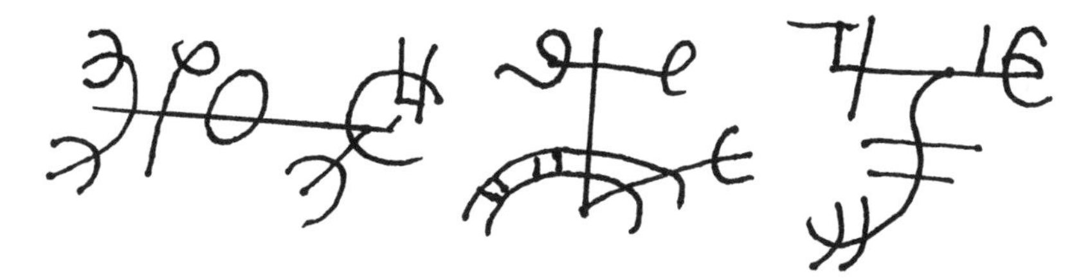

*This is a garbled representation of part of the Paternoster formula (see appendix D, pg. 124).

## VIII. SLEEP MAGIC

The lore of sleep and dreams runs deep in Icelandic magic. Here are some spells relating to the magic of sleep and dreams.

### 1 ❄ Lucid Dreaming—Dream Stave I (Davíðsson XV)

Carve this sign on fir wood and sleep upon it; then you will dream whatever you want.

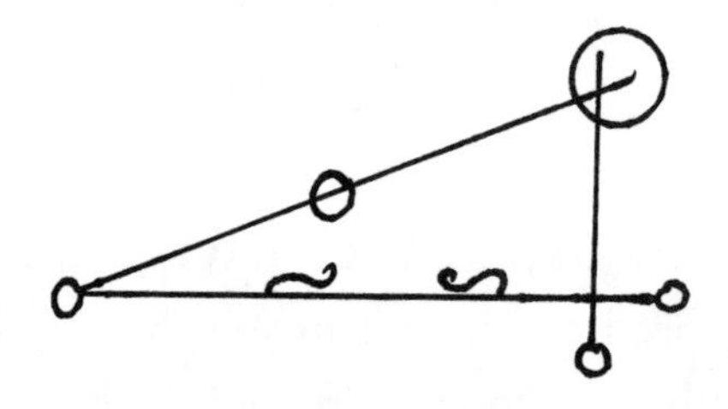

### 2 ❄ Dream Sendings—Dream Stave II (Davíðsson XVI)

Carve this sign on so-called oak wood and without your subject knowing it, lay it under the head of the one who should receive dreams according to what it is you want him or her to dream about.

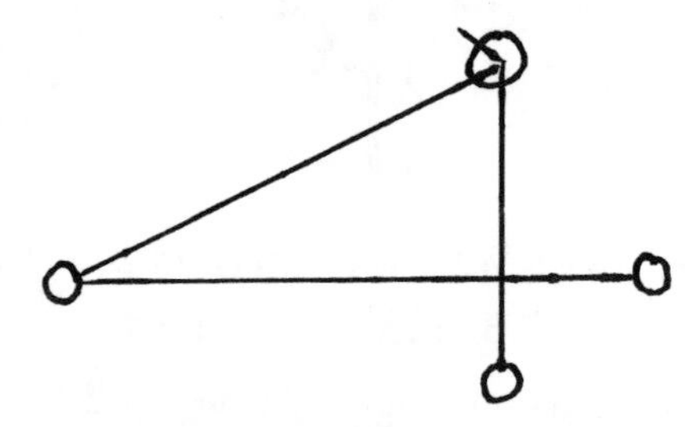

### 3 ❄ Against Headache and Insomnia (*Galdrabók* 5)

Write the following verse against headache and sleep disturbances and put it in your nightcap or under your head or under the head of the sufferer. When you or the sufferer go to sleep, the situation will be improved: *Milant vá vitaloth jebóa feboath.**

*The last two words of this formula are obvious misspellings or variants of the name Jehovah Sebaoth (Yahweh Tzabaoth), the ancient Hebrew war god. The first three words of the formula may be names of God connected by the Hebrew word for "and" (*vé*). These names also occur in a Swedish spell for headaches (see Lindqvist, *En isländsk Svartkonstbok från 1500-talet,* 28).

## *APPENDIX A*
# Runes and Magical Letters

One of the greatest errors made by some who try to make sense of galdor staves and their connections to runes stems from their attempts to use the Older Fuþąrk of twenty-four runes to analyze the staves. The older system would not have been known to the galdor men of Iceland. They would have known about the Younger Fuþąrk, the Runic Alphabet, and various systems of *galdraletur* ("magical letters") such as those reproduced in the lists of letters and their lore in appendix C. Although the Runic Alphabet was used for most representations of natural language in the magical literature, the lore of the sixteen-rune Younger Fuþąrk remained in the awareness of learned men. We know this because the Rune Poems are restricted to the lore and order of that system.

TABLE 1. THE YOUNGER RUNE ROW

| Number | Shape | Phonetic Value | Name | Meaning of Name |
|---|---|---|---|---|
| 1 | ᚠ | f | *fé* | money, gold, livestock |
| 2 | ᚢ | u/o | *úr* | drizzle, slag |
| 3 | ᚦ | th | *þurs* | giant (thurs) |
| 4 | ᚬ | ą | *áss* | a god (or estuary) |
| 5 | ᚱ | r | *reið* | riding |

TABLE 1. THE YOUNGER RUNE ROW (con't.)

| Number | Shape | Phonetic Value | Name | Meaning of Name |
|---|---|---|---|---|
| 6 | ᚴ | k/g | *kaun* | sore, ulcer |
| 7 | ᚼ | h | *hagall* | "hail" (special runic name) |
| 8 | ᚾ | n | *nauð(r)* | need, distress |
| 9 | ᛁ | i/e | *íss* | ice |
| 10 | ᛅ | a | *ár* | good year, harvest |
| 11 | ᛋ | s | *sól* | sun |
| 12 | ᛏ | t/d | *Týr* | (the god) Týr |
| 13 | ᛒ | b/p | *bjarkan* | birch twig |
| 14 | ᛘ | m | *maðr* | man, human |
| 15 | ᛚ | l | *lögr* | water |
| 16 | ᛦ | -r/y | *ýr* | yew (bow) |

TABLE 2. THE MEDIEVAL NORSE RUNIC ALPHABET

| Rune | Letter | Commentary on Form |
|---|---|---|
| ᛆ | a | Younger Fuþąrk **a** |
| ᛒ | b | Younger Fuþąrk **b** |
| ᛍ | c | Variant of z |
| ᛑ | d | Dotted Younger Fuþąrk **t** |
| ᛂ | e | Dotted Younger Fuþąrk **i** |
| ᚠ | f | Younger Fuþąrk **f** |
| ᚵ | g | Dotted Younger Fuþąrk **k** |
| ᚼ | h | Younger Fuþąrk **h** |
| ᛁ | i/j | Younger Fuþąrk **i** |
| ᚴ | k | Younger Fuþąrk **k** |
| ᛚ | l | Younger Fuþąrk **l** |
| ᛘ | m | Younger Fuþąrk **m** |
| ᚿ | n | Younger Fuþąrk **n** |
| ᚮ | o | Based on Younger Fuþąrk **ą** |
| ᛔ | p | Dotted Younger Fuþąrk **b** |
| ᚴ | q | Younger Fuþąrk **k** |

| Rune | Letter | Commentary on Form |
|---|---|---|
| ᚱ | r | Younger Fuþąrk **r** |
| ᛌ | s/z | Younger Fuþąrk **s** |
| ᛐ | t | Younger Fuþąrk **t** |
| ᚦ | þ | Younger Fuþąrk **þ** |
| ᚢ | u/v/w | Younger Fuþąrk **u** |
| ᛦ | R/y | Younger Fuþąrk **-R** (*ýr*) |
| ᚤ | y | Dotted Younger Fuþąrk **u** |
| ᛧ | z | Variant of c |
| ᛆ | æ | Younger Fuþąrk **a** (variant of ᛅ) |
| ᚯ | ø | Based on Younger Fuþąrk **ą** |

## TABLE 3. RULES FOR TRANSLITERATING NAMES INTO RUNES

| Vowels | | Consonants | |
|---|---|---|---|
| a/á | ᛆ | b/p | ᛒ |
| ö | ᛆᚢ or ᛆ | (c) (q) | ᚴ |
| ø | ᚢ or ᛆᚢ | k/g, ng | |
| ei/ey | ᛆᛁ | l | ᛚ |
| æ/œ | ᛆ or ᛁ | m | ᛘ |
| æn/œn | ᚨ | n | ᚾ |
| o/ó | ᚢ | medial and initial r- | ᚱ |
| u/ú | ᚢ | th or þ, ð | ᚦ |
| e/é | ᛁ | final -r | ᛦ or ᚱ |
| y/ý | ᚢ | s/z | ᛊ |
| i/í | ᛁ | t/d | ᛏ |
| | | v | ᚢ |
| | | f | ᚠ |
| | | j | ᛁ |
| | | h | ᚼ |

Nasals (m/n) before dentals (d/t) are generally not written. Runes are generally not doubled. Rules such as these may be violated for magical purposes.

By way of example, if one wants to put the name Óðinn into runes, it would come out: ᚢᚦᛁᚾ. The name Fundinn would come out as ᚠᚢᛏᛁᚾ.

## APPENDIX B

# Names of Óðinn

Names of Óðinn can be used for operative purposes. Each has a meaning that reveals its area of magical function. The names can be first turned into runic formulas and then used as the bases of *galdramyndir.* Suggested operative aims appear in parentheses. This is not a complete list of the names of Óðinn, but it does contain the most magically useful ones.

***Aldaföðr:*** "Father of Men" [for workings affecting all of mankind]

***Aldagautr:*** "*Gautr* (Father) of Men" [for workings affecting all of mankind]

***Alföðr:*** "All-Father" [for workings affecting all of mankind]

***Arnhöfði:*** "Eagle Head," mythically referring to the theft of *Óðrœrir,* the mead of poetry [for inspiration and stealth]

***Atríðr:*** "The One Who Rides to Battle" [for aggressive magic]

***Auðun:*** "Wealth Friend" [for wealth]

***Báleygr:*** "Fire Eye" [for insight beyond Midgard]

***Bíldr:*** "Knife for Bloodletting" [works of healing]

***Björn:*** "Bear" [to gain strength]

***Blindr:*** "Blind" [to gain inner vision]

***Bölverkr:*** "Bale (Evil) Worker" [to gain cunning and be deceptive for the purposes of gain]

***Farmaguð:*** "Cargo God" [for good business or to help the dead cross to the other side]

***Farmatýr:*** "Cargo God" (same as *Farmaguð*)

***Fengr:*** Either "Booty" (see also *Farmaguð, Farmatýr*) or "The One Who Catches," referring to his collection of souls for Valhöll [for gaining riches, or for expression of loyalty to Óðinn]

***Fimbultýr:*** "The Great God" (*fimbul* is a high-level intensifier of meaning) [for general personal power]

***Fimbulþulr:*** "The Great Magical Speaker" [for eloquence]

***Fjallgeiguðr:*** "The One Who Travels over Fells (mountains)" [for aid in navigating through life's difficulties]

***Fjölnir:*** "The Concealer" (from *fela,* perhaps referring to the mead of poetry) [for empowering any magical work through concealment]

***Fjölsviðr:*** "The One Who Knows Much" [for works of enlightenment]

***Forni:*** "The Old One" [for discovery of primeval wisdom]

***Fornölvir:*** "Ancient Ølvir–Heathen Ølvir" (the name Ølvir may have originally meant "the very holy") [for sanctification of a person or place]

***Fráríðr:*** "Swift Rider" (this name may be related to Óðinn's role as the riding god of death; see also *Atríðr*) [for sendings]

***Fundinn:*** "The Found One" [for works of discovery of unknown things]

***Gagnráðr:*** "The One Who Advises Against," that is, "antagonist in an argument" [to win an argument or legal case]

***Gangráðr:*** "The One Who Knows the Way" [for seeking advice from a divine source on the directions one should take in life]

***Gapþrosnir:*** "The One Who Ripens Magical Signs" [for use in charging or loading signs]

***Gautr:*** "Gaut, Goth, Man from Gotland," also the name of the tribal father of the Gothic folk; clearly Óðinn's name as tribal patriarch [to strengthen bonds of identity with the noble ancestors]

***Geiguðr:*** "The One Swinging on the Gallows" [for works of personal transformation]

***Geirlöðnir:*** "The One Who Invites (to battle) with a Spear" [to express fearlessness]

***Geirtýr:*** "Spear God" [to learn the mysteries of the spear]

***Ginnarr:*** "Bewitcher, Deceiver, Sorcerer" are the usual definitions, but the name goes back to the original meaning: "He who Creates out of *Ginn* (the magically charged void)" [for any and all acts of creativity]

***Gizurr:*** Related to the Norse verb *geta,* denoting Óðinn's ability to solve riddles [for solving problems]

***Glapsviðr:*** "Used to Luring" [for works of seduction]

***Goðjaðarr:*** "Protector of the Gods" [for preserving the gods in the world]

***Göndlir:*** "Wand Bearer" (from *göndull,* "magical staff, magic wand" or "male member") [to seal processes of internal transformation]

***Grímnir:*** "The Masked" [for concealing your works, especially if they are aimed at enemies]

***Grímr:*** "The Masked" [for malevolent workings against enemies]

***Gunnblindi:*** "He Who Causes Blindness in Battle" [for causing confusion among your enemies]

***Hagvirkr:*** "Skillful Worker" [for focusing your skills]

***Hangaguð:*** "God of the Hanged" or "Hanged God" [for works of self-transformation]

***Hangatýr:*** "God of the Hanged" or "Hanged God" (same as *Hangaguð*)

***Hangi:*** "Hanged One" (same as *Hangaguð*)

***Haptaguð:*** "Fetter God" [can be used either to bind your enemies and make them helpless or to liberate yourself from inner fetters]

***Haptsonir:*** "Fetter Looser" [specifically for self-liberation from that which binds you, physically or magically]

***Hárr:*** "The High One" [to honor the High One]

***Harr or Hárr:*** "The One-Eyed," perhaps also "Gray-Haired" [either for works of self-sacrifice for the sake of transformation or to declare an initiatory state of wisdom]

***Herföðr:*** "Host Father" [for organizing people to a common cause]

***Herteitr:*** "Host Glad" [to gather people to a common cause]

***Her-Týr:*** "Host God" [to make one's self a good organizer]

***Hjálmberi:*** "Helm Bearer" [for protection]

***Hjarrandi:*** "The Rattler" (this is a reference to the sound made by a raven) [for workings related to raven magic, that is, communication and intellectual synthesis]

***Hnikarr:*** "Instigator" [to set processes in motion]

***Hrafnáss:*** "Raven God" [for works in gaining wisdom]

***Hrafnaguð:*** "Raven God" [for works in gaining wisdom]

***Hrani:*** "The Rough One," or "The Uncultivated" [for works in defiance of conventional restraints]

***Hrjótr:*** "The Roarer" [for works of ecstasy]

***Hroptatýr:*** "The Hidden God" [to know the unknown]

***Hroptr:*** "The Hidden One" [to know the unknown]

***Hvatmóðr:*** "Rash Courage" [for works of courage]

***Itrekr:*** "Excellent Ruler" [to govern, manage, or lead well]

***Jafnhár:*** "Just as High" [to declare an initiatory state of wisdom]

***Jalfaðr, Jölfuðr:*** "Yellow-Brown Bear" [for works of strength]

***Járngrímr:*** "Iron cruel" [to cause strife]

***Jólnir:*** "Leader of the Yule Beings (gods)" (Óðinn is called Jólnir because he is particularly worshipped at Yule) [to be contemplated at the Yuletide]

***Jörmunr:*** "The Great One" [for especially great undertakings]

***Njótr:*** "Enjoyer, User" [to gain comfort and well-being]

***Óðinn:*** "Master of Inspiration" [for all kinds of work]

***Óðr:*** "Poetic Inspiration" [for gaining inspiration]

***Ófnir:*** "Inciter" or "Combative Weaver" (used for a snake in *Grímnismál* 34, probably referring to Óðinn's metamorphosis into a snake) [for works of inner transformation intended to serve the greater community]

***Ómi:*** "The Resonant Voiced," or, more likely, "The Highest" [for acts of worship or praise of the divinity]

***Óski:*** "Wished for" [for getting a wish fulfilled]

***Rögnir:*** "Divine One" or "Ruler of the *Regin* (gods)" [for acts of worship or praise of the divinity]

***Sangetall:*** "Obtaining the Truth" [for learning the truth]

***Sannr/Saðr:*** "The True One, the Sooth" [for learning the truth]

***Sigfaðir or Sigföðr:*** "Victory Father" [for obtaining victory or success]

***Siggautr:*** "Victory Gautr" [for obtaining victory or success]

***Sigmundr:*** "Victory Protection" [for protecting the fruits of victory]

***Sigtryggr:*** "Victory Trustee" [for success in all things, especially conflicts]

***Sigtýr:*** "Victory God" [for success in all things, especially conflicts]

***Skollvaldr:*** "Ruler of Treachery or Cunning" [to become cunning]

***Sváfnir:*** "Slayer or 'Putter to Sleep,'" (the name of a snake in *Grímnismál* 34) [for curses or to cause someone to lose awareness]

***Sviðrir:*** "The Enlightener" [for works of enlightenment]

***Svipall:*** "Swift Moving/Changeable" [for works causing sudden changes in events]

***Unnr or Uðr:*** possibly "The Beloved" or the god of fellowship, from *vínr* [to make oneself popular]

***Vakr:*** "Awake" [for works of awakening to higher consciousness]

***Valföðr:*** "Father of the Slain" [for works of necromancy, to gain knowledge from the dead; this is the use of most of the names beginning with the element *Val-*]

***Valgautr:*** "Gautr of the Slain" [to honor ancestors or for works of gaining knowledge from them]

***Valkjósandi:*** "Chooser of the Slain" [to help the dead pass the Rainbow Bridge happily]

***Valtamr:*** "Accustomed to the Slain" [to honor ancestors or for works of gaining knowledge from them]

***Valtýr:*** "God of the Slain" [to honor ancestors or for works of gaining knowledge from them]

***Valþögnir:*** "Receiver of the Slain" [to help the dead pass the Rainbow Bridge happily]

***Vegtamr:*** "Accustomed to the Road" [for works of transformation or travel]

***Veratýr:*** "God of Men" [for works to affect one's fellow men]

***Viðrir:*** "Weather Causer" [for weather magic]

***Viðurr:*** "Annihilator, Slayer" [for works of vengeance]

***Vingnir:*** "The Swinger/Striker/Turner" [to attack enemies]

***Víðfrægr:*** "Wide Famed" [to make one's fame greater]

***Vöfuðr:*** "Hanger/Dangler" [for self-transformation]

***Yggr:*** "The Terrible" [to persevere through hard times toward transformation]

***Þekkr:*** "Comfortable, Beloved" [to gain a good spouse]

***Þrasarr:*** "The Quarreler, the Angry" [to cause fear in enemies]

***Þrór:*** "The Successful" [for success in all things]

***Þróttr:*** "Strength" [for strength]

## APPENDIX C

# Magical Letters and Rune Kennings

Here are eight lists of magical letters. Each letter has a phonetic value linked to the adapted Roman alphabet used to write the Scandinavian languages in the Middle Ages. These are magical letter substitutes for those ordinary letters. Each of them was also given a kenning, or special interpretive phrase, that said something about the meaning or symbolic value of the letter. These kennings are usually linked to the lore of the runes used in the ancient North. The letters can be used to write magical missives—correspondence addressed to the powers of magic to gain certain effects. Such characters can also be used to conceal the meaning of texts, or specific words or passages in them, from the eyes of the uninitiated. Most important, however, they can be used as secret encodings in the constructions of magical signs. Magical signs can be created from their forms, just as runes are used. They can also be used as flourishes in such signs. I invite you to discover their mysteries, whosoever can.

## LIST I

| Letter | Kenning | Translation |
|---|---|---|
| a | *Gumna gaman* | "pleasure of man" |
| b | *Vallar-fax* | "field's mane" (forest) |
| c | *Folin sunna* | "hidden sun" |
| d | *Kórmundur* | "choir bride's price" |
| e | *Stunginn unnar hlemmr* | "dotted/pointed wave cover" |
| f | *Virðingar-efni* | "valuable substance" |
| g | *Kona Héðins* | "*Héðin's wife*" |
| h | *Þruma hlýrs* | "thunder of mildness" |
| i | *Jarðar-bann* | "earth's restriction" |
| k | *Varna nauð* | "distress of the defenses" |
| l | *Þröngvasti kostur* | "most difficult choice" |
| m | *Bóknáms-byrlir* | "book learnings" |
| n | *Hunda-mál* | "speech of dogs" |
| o | *Flóðs-fæða* | "food of the flood" |
| p | *Norna-sviði* | "burning pain inflicted by Norns" |
| q | *Hildar-högg* | "stroke of battle" |
| r | *Úlfalda-rás* | "Camel's race" |
| s | *Landa-skjal* | "lands' deed" |
| t | *Baldur meiddr* | "Baldur injured" |
| u | *Vinds-hæli* | "winds' shelter" |
| x | *Vinda-flegða* | "wind's giantess" |
| y | *Uppdreginn álmr* | "pulled-up elm-tree" |
| z | *Mundar-fegra* | "bride-price's beauty" |
| þ | *Kvenna-ból* | "women's abode" (mistake for *böl*, "bale, misfortune"?) |

## LIST II

| Letter | Kenning | Translation |
|---|---|---|
| a | *Jarðar-gróði* | "earth's increase/growth" |
| b | *Vor-hrím* | "spring rime" |
| c | *Knje-Freyja* | "knee lady" (*kné* = "degree of relationship") |
| d | *Kærleiki* | "love, charity" |
| e | *Brostið keldulok* | "broken well-lid" |
| f | *Hljóðlæti manns* | "stillness/silence of a man" |
| g | *Högnadóttir* | "tomcat's daughter" |
| h | *Mari himna* | "bedpost of the heavens" |
| i | *Ár-börkur* | "river's bark" |
| k | *Manna-tjón* | "men's loss/damage" |
| l | *Ekrurúm* | "acre-bed" |
| m | *Skipa-skreytir* | "ship's ornamentation" |
| n | *Eggja-broddnagli* | "edged spike-nail" |
| o | *Valhallar-vísir* | "Valhalla's director" |
| p | *Rauna-fró* | "tried-and-true relief/comfort" |
| r | *Skimners-mæði* | "exhaustion/weariness of the shining one" |
| s | *Landa-birta* | "lands' brightness" |
| t | *Fræhverfa* | "seed return" |
| u | *Skjalda-fundr* | "shields' meeting/fight" (war) |
| x | *Bjarkar-hyrja* | "birch's giantess" (cf. Hyrja in the *þulur* of the *Prose Edda*) |
| y | *Fugla-sjón* | "bird's sight" (bird's-eye view) |
| z | *Mundar-sunna* | "bride-price's sun" |
| þ | *Raumur* | "giant" (cf. Raumr in the *þulur* of the *Prose Edda*), "big, clownish person" |
| æ | *Skipa-byr* | "ship's wind" (good or fair wind for sailing) |

## LIST III

| Letter | Kenning | Translation |
|---|---|---|
| a | *Engi, tún* | "meadowland; farmstead" |
| b | *Viðar-ull* | "wood's wool" (cotton?) |
| c | *Hné hróður* | "knee praise; fame; reputation" |
| d | *Feddur þórs bur* | "born Thor's son" |
| e | *Stunginn bekkja stokkr* | "pointed bench stock" |
| f | *Tólf saman* | "twelve together" (dozen) |
| g | *Manns vera* | "a man's shelter, dwelling" |
| h | *Himna salt* | "heavens' salt" |
| i | *Bekkja stokkr* | "bench stock" |
| k | *Barna-böl* | "children's bale/misfortune" |
| l | *Ymis blóð* | "Ymir's blood" |
| m | *Hláturs-efni* | "laughter's stuff" |
| n | *Sorgar-sögur* | "sorrow tales" (tragedies) |
| o | *Fiska-dvöl* | "short stay of fish" |
| p | *Symsla-lækning* | "ointment medicine" |
| q | *Bentur bogi* | "bent bow" |
| r | *Léttfeta rás* | "light-footed race" |
| s | *Hjóla-haukur* | "wheel hawk" |
| t | *Úlfsgin* | "wolf's jaws" |
| u | *Hirðis hatur* | "shepherd's hate" |
| x | *Baldur* | "the god Baldur" |
| y | *Mundar-sýn* | "bride-price's sun" |
| þ | *Skrumnir* | "swaggerer" (also name for a raven) |
| æ | *Sifja-reynir* | "examiner of affinity" |

## LIST IV

| Letter | | Kenning | Translation |
|---|---|---|---|
| a | | *Gott sumar* | "good summer" |
| b | | *Bjarka ull* | "birch wool" |
| c | | *Kné sýn* | "knee sun" |
| d | | *Meiddur hlýri Þórs* | "wounded (twin) brother of Thor" (Baldur) |
| e | | *Jökuls auga* | "glacier's eye" |
| f | | *Peninga sjóður* | "moneybag" |
| g | | *Handar-ljós* | "hand's light" |
| h | | *Himna-malt* | "heavens' malt" |
| i | | *Unnar-þekja* | "wave's roof" |
| k | | *Hildur* | "battle" |
| l | | *Lygruband* | "liar's fetter" (restricter of lies) |
| m | | *Moldar auki* | "increase of mold" (earth) |
| n | | *Ofraun* | "too great a trial, too great a test" |
| o | | *Manns-mynd* | "a man's image" |
| p | | *Gott líf* | "good life" |
| r | | *Gota skref* | "Gothic [here a poetic term = horse's] step, pace, stride" |
| s | | *Hróður* | "praise; fame, reputation" |
| t | | *Úlfs-leyfar* | "wolf's leavings" (a kenning for Týr in the Old Icelandic Rune Poem) |
| u | | *Þurka-bann* | "ban of dryness, draught" (*bann* = rain) |
| x | | Genja | "ax" |
| y | | *Bardaga-gagn* | "battle benefit" |
| þ | | *Fornjötur* | "old giant" (or "old mangers"?) |

## LIST V

| Letter | Kenning | Translation |
|---|---|---|
| a | *Algróinn akur* | "grown-up field" |
| b | *Laufgaður viður* | "leafy tree" |
| c | *Ilur jöfur* | "bad boar [king]" |
| d | *Úlfs-fóstri* | "wolf's foster-father or son" |
| e | *Brotinn ís* | "broken ice" |
| f | *Opin vök* | "open hole (in the ice)" |
| g | *Kíla-kvöl* | "suffering from boils" |
| h | *Krapa-drífa* | "sleet-fall, shower of sleet" |
| i | *Straums-fjöl* | "stream's plank" |
| k | *Barna-böl* | "children's bale/misfortune" |
| l | *Skipa-fold* | "ship's field" |
| m | *Þungur kostr* | "difficult choice (situation)" |
| n | *Missir fjár* | "loss of money" |
| o | *Lýða-fæða* | "(common) people's food" |
| p | *Kviðr-bót* | "verdict compensation" (legal remedy) |
| q | *Hildar-högg* | "battle's stroke" |
| r | *Snúðug för* | "swift journey" |
| s | *Suðra-bákn* | "southern beacon" |
| t | *Einhendr Ás* | "one-handed god" |
| u | *Skýja grátur* | "clouds' weeping" |
| y | *Skotmanns ör* | "shooter's/harpooner's scar" |
| þ | *Þursa bit* | "thurses' bite" |
| æ | *Fastur örn* | "steadfast eagle" |
| ö | *Ørfa-mælir* | "generous measure" |

## LIST VI

| Letter | Kenning | Translation |
|---|---|---|
| a | *Fugla-fögnuður* | "birds' good cheer" |
| b | *Skógar-lim* | "forest's branch" |
| c | *Sólar-ris* | "sun's rise" |
| d | *Særður jarðarsonur* | "wounded [pointed] earth son" |
| e | *Særður unnarhlemmr* | "wounded [pointed] wave cover" |
| f | *Vinur höfðingja* | "friend of chieftains" |
| g | *Handarmein* | "a sore in the hand" |
| h | *Himna þruma* | "heavens' thunder" |
| i | *Vatna þil* | "waters' covering" |
| k | *Bardagi* | "battle" (cf. Old Icelandic Rune Poem) |
| l | *Landa-belti* | "land's belt" (surrounding sea) |
| m | *Raunabót* | "true/real bettering" |
| n | *Þjónustusínkur maður* | "service-stingy man" |
| o | *Svana-grund* | "swans' (green) field" |
| p | *Valt líf* | "easily upset life" |
| r | *Sitjandi sæla* | "a blessing to the one sitting" |
| s | *Skýja-skjöldur* | "clouds' shield" |
| t | *Øfugstreymi* | "awkward stream" (crosscurrent) |
| u | *Viðar-flegða* | "wood giantess" |
| y | *Bentur bogi* | "a bent bow" |
| þ | *Kvennaval* | "women's choice" |
| ö | *Soðketill við eld* | "cooking kettle on the fire" |

## LIST VII

| Letter | Kenning | Translation |
|---|---|---|
| a | *Siglufákur á ferð* | "mast's horse [ship] on a journey" |
| b | *Ljómi viðar* | "radiance of a tree" |
| c | *Fullur máni* | "full moon" |
| d | *Úlfs ben* | "(the) wolf's wound" |
| e | *Vatna-feldur* | "waters' cloak" |
| f | *Metorð manns* | "valuation/rank of a man" |
| g | *Kíla-kvöl* | "suffering from boils" |
| h | *Himna-grjót* | "heavens' gravel/stones" |
| i | *Sela-sæng* | "seal's bed" |
| k | *Bardaga sár* | "battle/beating wound" |
| l | *Glanna-gólf* | "reckless jester's floor" |
| m | *Sverða-bör* | "swords' tree" (*börr* = tree) |
| n | *Sjónleysi* | "sight dissolution" (blindness) |
| o | *Kópa-róma* | "(young) seal's clash/battle" |
| p | *Smurning ákomu* | "annointing arrival" (extreme unction?) |
| r | *Skyndi-ferð* | "speedy journey" |
| s | *Ymis-auga* | "Ymir's eye" (the sun) |
| t | *Banda-vagn* | "Fetters' [gods'] vehicle" (astronomical = Ursa Major) |
| u | *Akra-yndi* | "fields' delight" |
| x | *Loka-ráð* | "Loki's plan/counsel" |
| y | *Stutt fjör* | "short life" |
| z | *Völvusæti* | "the völva's seat" |
| þ | *Þrúðvangur* | "doughty field" (abode of Thor) |
| æ | *Silfur-sjóður* | "silver moneybag" |

## LIST VIII

| Letter | | Kenning | Translation |
|---|---|---|---|
| a | ᛅ | *fugla söngur* | "birds' song" |
| b | ᛒ | *Breiðablik* | "broad view" (abode of Baldur; cf. *Grímnismál* 12) |
| c | ᛍ | *Illur ármaður* | "bad steward" |
| d | ᛑ | *Samaður rómuvöndur* | "(well-) fitted clash-wand [sword]" |
| e | ᛂ | *Glugga-svell* | "window ice" |
| f | ᚠ | *Firða-rögur* | "warrior's strife" |
| g | ᚵ | *Fölar fréttir* | "pale news" |
| h | ᚼ | *Hrím skýja* | "rime of the clouds" |
| i | ᛁ | *Feigsfar* | "a doomed man's journey" |
| k | ᚴ | *Vígsben* | "war's wound" |
| l | ᛚ | *Humra-kvöld* | "twilight evening" |
| m | ᛘ | *Vinnu-sprengur* | "work bursting" |
| n | ᚾ | Sólsetur | "sunset" |
| o | ᚮ | *Álftalón* | "swans' sea inlet" |
| p | ᛔ | *Græðing meina* | "healing of injuries" |
| r | ᚱ | *Alinn hestur* | "(well-)maintained horse" |
| s | ᛋ | *Lyða-ljós* | "(common) people's light" |
| t | ᛏ | *Ylja-æti* | "warm oats" |
| u | ᚢ | *Æfistig* | "life rung (as of a ladder)" |
| y | ᚤ | *Spentur álmur* | "a drawn elm bow" |
| þ | ᚦ | *Þursa-raun* | "thurses' trial/ordeal" |
| ö | ᚯ | *Ør á flugi* | "arrow in flight" |

# APPENDIX D
# The "Our Father" Prayer in Latin

Often traditional formulas indicate that a magical sign is to be sanctified with the recitation of the "Our Father" prayer. As noted in the historical section, this prayer actually seems to predate any organized Christian Church activity. It appears to stem from the older school to which Jesus belonged and which taught the fatherhood of God. This was probably a school of ultimately Persian origin that taught the natural Indo-European idea of God as the actual progenitor of mankind. The so-called Lord's Prayer, or Paternoster, has a deep history in the annals of Germanic magic.

> *Pater noster, qui es in caelis, sanctificetur nomen tuum. Adveniat regnum tuum. Fiat voluntas tua, sicut in caelo et in terra. Panem nostrum quotidianum da nobis hodie, et dimitte nobis debita nostra sicut et nos dimittimus debitoribus nostris. Et ne nos inducas in tentationem, sed libera nos a malo. Amen.*

# Bibliography


Árnason, Jón. *Íslenzkar Þjóðsögur og Æfintýri*. Edited by Arni Bóðvarsson and Bjarni Viljálmsson. 6 vols. Second edition. Reykjavík: Þjóðsaga Prentsmiðjan Hólar, 1961.

Becker, Alfred. *Franks Casket*. Regensburg: Hans Carl, 1973.

Beckers, Hartmut. "Eine spätmittelalterliche deutsche Anleitung zur Teufelsbeschwörung mit Runenschriftverwendung." *Zeitschrift für deutsche Altertumskunde und deutsche Literatur* 113, no. 2 (1984): 136–45.

Burnett, Charles S. F., and Marie Stoklund. "Scandinavian Runes in a Latin Magical Treatise." *Speculum* 58, no. 2 (1983): 419–29.

Byock, Jesse, trans. *The Saga of the Volsungs*. London: Penguin, 1999.

Cleasby, Richard, and Gudbrand Vigfússon, eds. *An Icelandic-English Dictionary*. Second edition. Oxford: Clarendon Press, 1957.

Davíðsson, Ólafur. "Isländische Zauberzeichen und Zauberbücher." *Zeitschrift des Vereins für Volkskunde* 13 (1903): 150–67, 267–79; Tables III–VII. English version: *Icelandic Magic Symbols and Spell Books*. Translated and annotated by Justin Foster. www.academia.edu (accessed July 17, 2015).

Davies, Owen. *Grimoires: A History of Magic Books*. Oxford and New York: Oxford University Press, 2009.

Dickins, Bruce, ed. *Runic and Heroic Poems of the Old Teutonic Peoples*. Cambridge: Cambridge University Press, 1915.

Dillmann, François-Xavier. *Les magiciens dans l'Islande ancienne*. Diss. doctorat d'Etat. Caen: University of Caen, 1986.

Dumézil, Georges. *Gods and Myths of the Ancient Northmen*. Edited by Einar Haugen. Berkeley: University of California Press, 1973.

Einarsson, Stefán. *A History of Icelandic Literature.* New York: Johns Hopkins Press, 1957.

Elliott, Ralph. *Runes: An Introduction.* Second edition. New York: St. Martin's Press, 1989.

Ellis (Davidson), H. R. *Gods and Myths of Northern Europe.* Harmondsworth, U.K.: Penguin, 1964.

———. "Hostile Magic in the Icelandic Sagas." In *The Witch Figure,* edited by V. Newell, 20–41. London: Routledge and Kegan Paul, 1973.

———. *The Road to Hel.* Cambridge: Cambridge University Press, 1943.

Falk, Hjalmar. *Odensheite.* Kristiania [Oslo]: Dybwad, 1924.

Flowers, Stephen E. *The Galdrabók: An Icelandic Book of Magic.* Second revised edition. Smithville, Tex.: Rûna-Raven, 2005.

———. *The Galdrabók: An Icelandic Grimoire.* York Beach, Me.: Weiser, 1989.

———. *Johannes Bureus and Adalruna.* Smithville, Tex.: Rûna-Raven, 1998.

———. *Runes and Magic.* New York: Lang, 1986.

———. *The Rune-Poems.* Smithville, Tex.: Rûna-Raven, 2002.

Foster, Justin. "The Huld Manuscript—ÍB 383 4to: A Modern Transcription, Decryption and Translation." Unpublished article on www.academia.edu (accessed 16 June 2015).

Gandee, Lee R. *Strange Experience.* Englewood Cliffs, N.J.: Prentice-Hall, 1971.

Gjerset, Knut. *History of Iceland.* New York: Macmillan, 1924.

Grimm, Jacob. *Teutonic Mythology.* Translated by James Steven Stalleybrass. 4 vols. New York: Dover, 1966.

Gustavson, Helmer, and Thorgunn Snaedal Brink. "Runfynd 1978." *Fornvännen* (1979): 228–50.

Hampp, Irmgard. *Beschwörung-Segen-Gebet: Untersuchungen zum Zauberspruch aus dem Bereich der Volkskunde.* Stuttgart: Silberburg, 1961.

Haraldsson, Erlendur. "Are We Sensitive or Superstitious?" *Icelandic Review* 17, no. 4 (1972): 30–34.

Hohman, John George. *The Long-Lost Friend: A 19th Century American Grimoire.* Edited by Daniel Harms. Woodbury, Minn.: Llewellyn, 2012.

Hollander, Lee M., trans. *The Poetic Edda.* Second edition. Austin: University of Texas Press, 1973.

Jones, Gwyn. *A History of the Vikings.* Second edition. London: Oxford University Press, 1984.

Jung, Erich. *Germanische Götter und Helden in christlicher Zeit.* Second edition. Munich: Lehmann, 1939.

Kålund, Kristian. *Den islandske lægebog.* Copenhagen: Luno, 1907.

Karlsson, Gunnar. *The History of Iceland.* Minneapolis: University of Minnesota Press, 2000.

Krause, Wolfgang. *Runen.* Berlin: De Gruyter, 1970.

Kuhn, Adalbert. "Indische und germanische Segensprüche." *Zeitschrift für vergleichende Sprachforschung* 13 (1864): 49–73.

Lecouteux, Claude. *The Book of Grimoires: The Secret Grammar of Magic.* Rochester, Vt.: Inner Traditions, 2013.

———. *Dictionary of Ancient Magic Words and Spells: From Abraxas to Zoar.* Rochester, Vt.: Inner Traditions, 2015.

Lindqvist, Natan. *En isländsk Svartkonstbok från 1500-talet.* Uppsala: Appelberg, 1921.

McKinnell, John, and Rudolf Simek, with Klaus Düwel. *Runes, Magic and Religion: A Sourcebook.* Vienna: Fassbaender, 2004.

Moeller, Walter O. *The Mithraic Origin and Meanings of the Rotas-Sator Square.* Leiden: Brill, 1973.

Pálsson, Hermann, and Paul Edwards, trans. *Egil's Saga.* Harmondsworth, U.K.: Penguin, 1976.

———, trans. *Eyrbyggja Saga.* Harmondsworth, U.K.: Penguin, 1976.

Rafnsson, Magnús. *Angurgapi: The Witch-Hunts in Iceland.* Hólmavík: Strandagaldur, 2003.

———, trans. *Rún: Galdrabók prentun á handriti af galdri og letri / A Facsimile of a Grimoire.* Hólmavík: Strandagaldur, 2014.

———, ed. *Tvær galdrabækur—Two Icelandic Books of Magic.* Hólmavík: Strandagaldur, 2008.

Rustad, Mary S., ed. and trans. *The Black Books of Elverum.* Lakeville, Minn.: Galde Press, 1999.

Sæmundsson, Matthías Viðar. *Galdrar á Íslandi: Íslensk galdrabók.* Oddi: Almenna Bókfélag, 1992.

Simpson, Jacqueline. *Icelandic Folktales and Legends.* Berkeley: University of California Press, 1972.

———. *Legends of Icelandic Magicians.* Cambridge, U.K.: Brewer, 1975.

Skuggi [Jochum M. Eggertson]. *Galdra-Skræða*. Privately printed, 1940. English edition: *Sorcerer's Screed: The Icelandic Book of Magic Spells*. Reykjavík: Lesstofan, 2015.

Smith, Christopher Alan. *Icelandic Magic: Aims, Tools and Techniques of the Icelandic Sorcerers*. Glastonbury, U.K.: Avalonia, 2015.

Solheim, Svale. "Draug." In *Kulturhistorisk leksikon for nordisk middelalder*, vol. 3, 297–99. Copenhagen: Rosenkilde og Bagger, 1958.

Ström, Folke. *Den döendes makt och Oden i trädet*. Gothenburg: Elander, 1947.

Strömbäck, Dag. *Sejd*. Stockholm: Geber, 1935.

Sturluson, Snorri. *Edda*. Translated by Anthony Faulkes. London: Dent, 1987.

———. *Heimskringla*. Translated by Lee M. Hollander. Second edition. Austin: University of Texas Press, 1962.

Thorsson, Edred [Stephen E. Flowers]. *The Nine Doors of Midgard: A Curriculum of Rune-Work*. Fifth revised and expanded edition. South Burlington, Vt.: Rune-Gild, 2015.

———. *Northern Magic*. Minneapolis: Llewellyn, 1992.

———. *Runelore*. York Beach, Me.: Weiser, 1987.

Turville-Petre, Edward Oswald Gabriel. *Myth and Religion of the North*. New York: Holt, Rinehart and Winston, 1964.

Vries, Jan de. *Altgermanische Religionsgeschichte*. 2 vols. Second edition. Berlin: De Gruyter, 1957.

# Index

Page numbers in *italics* indicate illustrations.
Page numbers followed by *t* indicate tables.

# Your Personal Magical Workings

## BOOKS OF RELATED INTEREST

**Rune Might**
The Secret Practices of the German Rune Magicians
*by Edred Thorsson*

**The Secret of the Runes**
by Guido von List
*Edited by Stephen E. Flowers*

**Nordic Runes**
Understanding, Casting,
and Interpreting the Ancient Viking Oracle
*by Paul Rhys Mountfort*

**Nightside of the Runes**
Uthark, Adulruna, and the Gothic Cabbala
*by Thomas Karlsson, Ph.D.*

**Runic Lore and Legend**
Wyrdstaves of Old Northumbria
*by Nigel Pennick*

**Pagan Magic of the Northern Tradition**
Customs, Rites, and Ceremonies
*by Nigel Pennick*

**Norse Goddess Magic**
Trancework, Mythology, and Ritual
*by Alice Karlsdottir*

**The Norse Shaman**
Ancient Spiritual Practices of the Northern Tradition
*by Evelyn C. Rysdyk*

**The Return of Odin**
The Modern Renaissance of Pagan Imagination
*by Richard Rudgley*

**Neolithic Shamanism**
Spirit Work in the Norse Tradition
*by Raven Kaldera and Galina Krasskova*

**Odin and the Nine Realms Oracle**
A 54-Card Set
*by Sonja Grace*

**Gods of the Runes**
The Divine Shapers of Fate
*by Frank Joseph*
*Illustrated by Ian Daniels*

**Encyclopedia of Norse and Germanic Folklore, Mythology, and Magic**
*by Claude Lecouteux*

**The Book of Grimoires**
The Secret Grammar of Magic
*by Claude Lecouteux*

**Russian Black Magic**
The Beliefs and Practices of Heretics and Blasphemers
*by Natasha Helvin*

**Slavic Witchcraft**
Old World Conjuring Spells and Folklore
*by Natasha Helvin*

Inner Traditions • Bear & Company
P.O. Box 388
Rochester, VT 05767
1-800-246-8648
www.InnerTraditions.com

Or contact your local bookseller